THE FIANCÉE CHARADE

BY
FIONA BRAND

Published in Great Britain 2013
by Mills & Boon, an imprint of Harlequin (UK) Limited,
Eton House, 18-24 Paradise Road, Richmond, Surrey TW9 1SR

© Fiona Gillibrand 2013

ISBN: 978 0 263 90476 5
ebook ISBN: 978 1 472 00611 0

51-0613

Harlequin (UK) policy is to use papers that are natural, renewable and recyclable products and made from wood grown in sustainable forests. The logging and manufacturing processes conform to the legal environmental regulations of the country of origin.

Printed and bound in Spain
by Blackprint CPI, Barcelona

Fiona Brand lives in the sunny Bay of Islands, New Zealand. Now that both her sons are grown, she continues to love writing books and gardening. After a life-changing time in which she met Christ, she has undertaken study for a bachelor of theology and has become a member of The Order of St. Luke, Christ's healing ministry.

Once again huge thanks to my editor, Stacy Boyd.

To the Lord, who helps and supports me in all things—especially writing. Thank you.

Come to me all you that are weary and are carrying heavy burdens, and I will give you rest. Take my yoke upon you, and learn from me; for I am gentle and humble in heart, and you will find rest for your souls.
—Matthew 11: 28, 29

One

Zane Atraeus Dates Good-time Girl....

The tabloid headline halted billionaire banker and entrepreneur Gabriel Messena in his tracks.

A subtle tension gripped him as he paid the attendant at the Auckland International Airport newsstand and flipped the scandal sheet open to verify just which good-time girl, exactly, his wild cousin Zane Atraeus had been dating this time.

His gaze was drawn to the color photo that went with the story. Every muscle in his body tightened as he studied familiar Titian hair, creamy skin and dark eyes; a long, sensually curved body that possessed the engaging grace of a dancer.

Not just any woman, Gabriel thought with a bleak sense of inevitability as he studied the cheerful glint of Gemma O'Neill's gaze. Once again, Zane was dating *his* woman.

Emotion, sharp and clarifying, clenched his stomach

muscles and banded his chest. When he had first discovered that Zane was dating Gemma, he had checked out the situation and had been satisfied that the dating was on a strictly business level. Although, according to the tabloid, at some point *that* had changed.

The attraction Zane felt for Gemma was a no-brainer. She was gorgeous and smart, with an impulsive nature and a fascinating bluntness that had captivated Gabriel when she had worked on the Messena estate as a gardener. Although, he couldn't understand what drew Gemma, who had never seemed to be the A-list party-girl type, to his younger, wilder cousin.

Jaw taut, he examined the fierce sense of possession that gripped him, the powerful desire to claim Gemma as his own, despite the fact that he hadn't seen her in almost six years. His growing fury that Zane, who had women lining up—and, apparently, enough time in his schedule to date them all—just couldn't seem to leave his former personal assistant alone.

Damn, he thought mildly. He had no problem identifying the emotion that held him in thrall, destroying his normal clarity. He was jealous of Zane: searingly, primitively jealous.

It was an emotion that made no sense given the length of time that had passed and the fact that what he and Gemma had shared had been nothing more than a steamy encounter that had spanned a few incandescent hours.

Hours that were still etched in his memory because they were literally the last fling of his carefree youth. Two days later his father had been killed in a car accident along with his mistress, the beautiful Katherine Lyon, a woman who had also happened to be the family housekeeper.

Amidst the grief and the scandal, the responsibility of managing the family bank, his volatile family and the

Thanks for
reading, here's
20% OFF your
next order!

millsandboon.co.uk

20% OFF*

with code
THANKSJUN

Visit www.millsandboon.co.uk today to get this exclusive offe

Ordering online is easy:

- 1000s of stories converted to eBook
- Big savings on titles you may have missed in store

Visit today and enter the code **THANKSJUN** at the checkout today to receive **20% OFF** your next purchase of books and eBooks*. You could be settling down with your favourite authors in no time!

media had descended on Gabriel's shoulders like a lead weight. Any idea that he should echo his father's disastrous mistake by continuing a liaison with an employee, no matter how attractive, had been shelved.

Until now.

Frowning at the sudden sharp desire to pick up the threads of a relationship that had its basis in the same kind of obsessive fatal attraction that had brought his father to ruin, Gabriel refolded the paper.

Strolling to the first-class counter, he checked his luggage and handed his passport to the attendant. While he waited for his boarding pass, he glanced again at the sketchy article, which also chronicled a number of Zane's fiery liaisons. Affairs that Zane had apparently been conducting with other women while he had kept Gemma on the back burner.

Intense irritation gripped him at the idea that Gemma had clearly thrown away her pride and reputation in favor of pursuing Zane. That she would allow herself to be treated as some kind of standby date. It just didn't gel with the strong streak of independence that had always been such an attractive part of her personality.

His gaze snagged on a phrase that made every muscle lock tight. Suddenly, the anomaly in Gemma's behavior was crystal-clear.

She was no longer strictly single. At some point in the past couple of years, she'd had a child. Presumably, Zane's child.

Taking a measured breath, Gabriel forced the humming tension from his muscles, although there was nothing he could do about the slam of his heart, or the curious hollow feeling as he grappled with the information.

Too late to wish that he had listened to what the tabloids had been blaring for almost two years. That at some point,

Zane had decided that having Gemma as his PA had not been enough, that he had installed her in his bed, as well.

He jerked at his dark blue silk tie, needing air. He needed to refocus, to reassert the control he'd worked so hard to instill in himself in place of the hot-blooded, passionate streak that was the bane of all Messena men. But something about the sheer intimacy of Gemma bearing a child cut deep. The fact that the child belonged to Zane, his own cousin, rubbed salt in the wound.

It was an intimacy that Gabriel, at age thirty, hadn't had time for in his life, and which was not in his foreseeable future.

But Zane, with all the irresponsibility of youth, had experienced that intimacy. And now, evidently, he no longer wanted the woman whom he had bound to him with a child.

But Gabriel did.

The thought dropped through the turmoil of his emotions like a stone dropping through cool, clear water.

Six years had passed. But in that moment the stretch of time barely registered. He felt like a sleeper waking up, all of his senses—the emotions he'd walked away from the night his father had died—flaring to intense, heated life.

He studied the photograph again, this time noting the way Gemma clung to Zane's arm, the relaxed intimacy of the pose.

A hot jolt of fury cleared away any reservations he might have had about claiming the woman he had walked away from in order to preserve his family and business.

Gemma had had a child. A baby.

Logic didn't alter his sense of disorientation, the disbelief that the pressures of business and his high-maintenance family had somehow blinded him and he had missed something…important.

Although the fact that he hadn't registered changes in Gemma's life shouldn't surprise him. Running an empire encumbered by an aging trustee who Gabriel now believed to be suffering from the early stages of dementia, in theory he didn't have time to sleep.

And he almost never had time for personal relationships. When he dated it was invariably for business or charity functions. The fact that he went home to an empty apartment every night he wasn't traveling hadn't bothered him.

Until now.

Taking his boarding pass with automatic thanks, he strolled through the busy airport, barely noticing the travelers jostling around him. In the midst of a crowd, it was an odd time to feel alone. An even odder time to examine the stark truth, that despite the constant demands on his time, his own personal life was as sterile and empty as a desert.

But that was about to change. He was on his way to the Mediterranean island of Medinos, the ancestral home of the Messena family. And the place where Gemma just happened to presently reside.

If he had a mystical streak, he would be tempted to say that the coincidence that he and Gemma would finally be together at the same location was kismet. But mysticism had never figured in the Messena psyche. Aside from the passionate streak, Messena men had another well-defined trait that went clear back to the Crusades. Ruthless and tactical, fighting for the Couer de Lion, Richard the Lionheart, they had flourished in battle, winning lands and fortresses. The habit of winning had been passed down a family line rich in sons, culminating in large holdings of land and enormous wealth.

Plundering was no longer in vogue. These days, Messena men usually leveraged what they wanted across boardroom tables, but the basic principle was still the same. Identify the objective, execute a plan, obtain the prize.

In this case the plan was simple: remove Gemma from Zane's clutches and install her back in *his* bed.

"Gabriel Messena…engaged before the month was out…"

The snatch of conversation flowing in off the sun-washed terrace of one of the Atraeus Resort's most luxurious suites stopped Gemma O'Neill in her tracks.

Her grip tightened on the tea tray she was carrying as fragments of the past surfaced like pieces of flotsam, taking her places that for six years she had refused to go, making her feel emotions she was usually very successful at avoiding.

A still bay, a clear midnight sky, studded with stars and pierced by a sickle moon. Gabriel Messena, his long, muscular body entwined with hers; hair dark as night, the cut of his cheekbones spare and faintly exotic, reminding her of crowded souks and the inky shadowed alcoves of Moorish palaces…

With an effort of will Gemma blinked away the too-vivid image, which was probably a result of being on Medinos, the kind of romantic destination that attracted newlyweds in droves.

Now, rattled instead of being simply on edge as she'd been before, she brought the trolley to a halt beside the dining table. The clatter attracted the attention of the two guests she had been tasked with settling in. They were VIPs in the most important sense of the word on Medinos, because they were close connections of the Atraeus family.

Although, in terms of Gemma's past, one of the guests was much more than that, even if Luisa Messena, Gabriel's mother, didn't seem to have a clue that the person serving afternoon tea and petit-fours was one of her ex-gardeners.

And her son's ex-lover.

Pasting a professional smile on her mouth, Gemma apologized, all the while keeping her face averted in the hope that she could hang on to her anonymity.

With crisp movements, she snapped a damask cloth open, settled it on the glossy little table then began the precision task of aligning plates and napkins. As she offloaded a carved silver teapot that was probably worth more than the car she needed to buy but as a single mother just couldn't afford, she fiercely wished she hadn't offered to give the hotel staff a hand with the influx of VIP guests.

"He's certainly waited for her long enough…she's perfect…. The family's wealthy, of course…."

Despite the fact that she was doing her level best not to listen, because as far as she was concerned Gabriel Messena was old history, Gemma's jaw locked on a surge of annoyance. Clearly Gabriel was on the point of proposing to some perfect preselected creature, probably a beautiful debutante who had been groomed and educated within an inch of her life and who was now finally ready for the wedding nuptials.

She ripped the tab off a bottle of chilled sparkling mineral water and tossed it in the little trash can on the bottom shelf of her trolley. A tinkling sound indicated that the tab had bounced off the side of the trash can and rolled onto the floor. Retrieving the tab, she placed it in the trash can with careful precision and poured mineral water into two glasses. Her jaw tightened as some sloshed over the side and soaked into her trolley cloth.

The knowledge that Gabriel was finally getting around to marriage after years of bachelorhood in the hushed stratosphere of enormous wealth in which he moved shouldn't have impacted her. She was happy for Gabriel. Perfectly, sublimely happy. She would have to remember to send him a congratulatory card.

She could do that, because she had moved on.

The conversation out on the terrace had segued from Gabriel to the more innocuous topic of shopping, which was a relief. Gemma guessed she couldn't hope to feel a complete absence of emotion about Gabriel, because as a teenager, he had been her focus; the man of her dreams. She had fallen in puppy love with him, and had mooned after him for years. Unfortunately she had been wasting her time because she hadn't had either the wealth or the family connections to be a viable part of his world.

One night, Gabriel had quenched the flare of passion that had bound them together as systematically as she imagined he would have vetoed an investment that lacked the required substance. He'd been polite, but he had made it clear they didn't have a future. He hadn't elaborated in any detail; he hadn't needed to. After the scandal that had hit the papers shortly after the one night they had spent together, Gemma had understood exactly why he had dropped her like the proverbial hot potato.

His father's affair with the family housekeeper had shaken the very foundations of the family banking business, which was based on wealthy clientele who were old-school and conservative. Gabriel had been in damage control mode. He hadn't wanted to inflame the scandal and undermine confidence in the bank any further by risking having his liaison with the gardener exposed to tabloid scrutiny.

Despite her heartache, Gemma had tried to see things from his perspective, to understand the battle he had faced. But the rejection, the knowledge that she had not been good enough to have a real, public relationship with Gabriel, had hurt in a way that had struck deep.

As soon as Gabriel had left after the short, awkward interview in which she had managed to remain superficially upbeat, she resolved to never look back or to even remember. It had been the emotional equivalent of sticking her head in the sand, but over the past six years, the tactic had worked.

Gemma took extra care transferring the bone china from the trolley to the table. Even so, an exquisitely delicate cup overturned on its saucer and a silver teaspoon that had been balanced on the saucer skidded off and hit a pretty bread and butter plate with a sharp ping.

She could feel the subtle tension and displeasure at the noise she was making. Her jaw set a fraction tighter. She had worked for the Atraeus Group for some years and normally didn't mind in the least helping out with any task that needed doing. The Atraeus family had given her a job when she desperately needed one, and they had treated her very well, but suddenly she was acutely aware of her role as a servant.

She dumped a glistening silver milk jug and sugar bowl down next to the teapot and swiped at an errant droplet of milk that marred the once pristine tablecloth.

Not that she had an issue with doing a good job, but it was a fact that she wasn't waitstaff. Just like she was no longer the gardener's daughter on the Messena estate.

She was a highly organized and well-qualified PA with a degree in performing arts on the side, and she was still trying to come to grips with the fact that by some errant trick of fate, she had ended up once more in the role of employee to a Messena.

Serene and perfectly groomed, Luisa looked exactly as she had when Gemma had last seen her in Dolphin Bay,

New Zealand. The friend accompanying her, though casually dressed, looked just as wealthy and well-groomed; her dark hair smooth, nails perfect. Unlike Gemma's hair, which she'd been too tired after a near-sleepless night on the phone to New Zealand to do anything with except to coil the heavy waves into a knot.

As she placed the crowning glory of the afternoon tea setting, an exquisite three-tiered plate of tiny cakes, scones, pastries and mini sandwiches, in the center of the table, she caught a glimpse of herself in a wall mirror.

She wasn't surprised that Luisa hadn't recognized her. The housemaid's smock she was wearing was at least a size too large and an unflattering pale blue, which leached all the color from her skin. With her hair pulled back into a severe knot, she didn't look either pretty or stylish.

Definitely not the gorgeous hothouse flower who by all accounts had been reserved for marriage to Gabriel, despite the fact that Gemma had borne his child.

The thought was overdramatic and innapropriate, and she regretted it the moment it was out.

She had cut her losses years ago, and from the snatches of conversation, Gabriel was practically engaged. If that was the case, then she was certain the manner in which he had selected his future bride had been as considered and measured as the way he managed the multibillion-dollar family business.

What had happened between her and Gabriel had been crazy and completely wrong for them both, a combination of moonlight and champagne, and a moment of chivalry when Gabriel had saved her from the groping of a too-amorous date.

By the time she had realized three months later, despite a couple of skimpy periods, that she was in fact pregnant, the decision to not tell Gabriel had been a no-brainer.

From the brief conversation that had taken place when Gabriel had told her he wasn't interested in a relationship, she had known that while he had been prepared to look after her and a baby if she had gotten pregnant, all he would have been doing was fulfilling an obligation. On that basis alone, she had chosen to take full responsibility for Sanchia. But there had been another driving force to staying silent about the baby.

Bearing a Messena child would have entailed links from which she would never have been free. She would have remained a beneficiary of Gabriel's family for the rest of her life, forever aware that she was the employee Gabriel Messena had made the mistake of getting pregnant but who hadn't been good enough to marry.

In the quiet solitude of her pregnancy, with the hurt of Gabriel's defection fading, Gemma had made the decision that in order to avoid more heartache, Sanchia would be hers and hers alone. Keeping her daughter's existence a secret had just seemed easier and simpler.

She straightened a cake fork. She guessed the part that made her hot under the collar about Gabriel's pending engagement was the idea that he had been waiting for his bride to become available. If that was the case, it meant that Gemma had never been anything more than a diversion, a fill-in, while he waited for the kind of wife he really wanted.

More memories cascaded, distracting her completely from her final check of the table setting.

The pressure of Gabriel's mouth on hers, the way his fingers had threaded in her hair...

Another pang of annoyance that Gabriel had given up on them so easily, that he was shallow and superficial enough to select a wife rather than fall passionately in love, started a sharp little throb at her temples. She wheeled the trolley with a little more force than was necessary to the door, clipping the side of a sofa in the process.

Luisa Messena, who was just walking in off the terrace, threw her a puzzled look, a frown pleating her brow, as if she was trying to remember where she had seen her last.

Bleakly, Gemma parked the trolley by the door and hoped Luisa didn't recall that it was the summer six years ago when she had thrown caution and every rule she'd lived by for years to the winds, and slept with Luisa's extremely wealthy son.

Jaw taut, in a blatant disregard for etiquette, Gemma didn't offer to pour the tea. Smiling blankly in the general direction of Luisa, she opened the door and pushed the trolley out into the hall.

Closing the door behind her, she drew a deep breath and wheeled the trolley toward the service elevator at the other end of the corridor, stopping short when her cell chimed.

Worry at the recognizable ringtone clutched at Gemma.

Checking that she wouldn't be overheard, she lifted the phone to her ear. Instantly, the too-serious voice of her five-year-old daughter filled her ears.

The conversation was punctuated by a regular *squeak-squeak* sound, which instantly translated an image of Sanchia clutching an old bedtime toy, a fluffy puppy with a squeezy sound in its tummy.

Gemma frowned, hating the distance between them when all she wanted to do was hug her close. Sanchia had clung to the toy as a baby, but these days she only ever picked it up if she was overtired or stressed.

Always precocious and older than her years, Sanchia had a familiar list of demands. She wanted to know where Gemma was and what she was doing, when she was coming to get her, exactly, and if she was bringing her a present.

There was a brief pause, then Sanchia's voice firmed as if she had finally reached the whole point of the conversation.

"And when are you bringing home the dad?"

Two

Gemma's heart sank. She had suspected that her daughter had overheard the discussion she'd had with Gemma's younger sister, Lauren, which had been half frivolous, half desperate. Now she had her proof.

The reference to "the dad" was heart-rending enough, as if obtaining a husband, and father for Sanchia, was as straightforward as shopping for shoes or a handbag.

Needing privacy even more now, Gemma walked down a short side hall while she tried to figure out what to say next.

Normally, she was composed, focused and highly organized. As a working single mother she'd had to be.

Although, lately, ever since disaster had struck in the form of a nanny who had left her daughter locked in the car while she gambled at a Sydney casino, Gemma's focus had undergone a quantum shift. A passerby had seen Sanchia and had called the police. Gemma had managed to explain her way out of the situation, but it hadn't helped that in the same week Gemma had also gotten caught up in a media scandal, courtesy of her connection with her ex-boss, Zane Atraeus.

To add insult to injury, when Gemma had dismissed the nanny, the woman had then turned around and sold a story to the papers claiming that Gemma was an unfit mother. The story, a collection of twisted truths and outright lies, hadn't exactly been front-page news, but because she had once worked for Zane, the gutter press had locked on to the story and run with it until another more juicy scandal had grabbed their attention.

Thankfully, the media attention had died, but the pressure from both Australian and New Zealand child welfare agencies hadn't, despite a number of interviews.

When she had tried to leave Australia with Sanchia for Medinos and her new job, the situation had taken a frightening turn. She had been accused of trying to escape before the welfare case was concluded and both she and Sanchia had been detained. Her mother had flown to Sydney to provide a stopgap answer by taking temporary custody of Sanchia and taking her home to New Zealand. But, to complicate matters, shockingly, her mother, who did not enjoy good health, had then had a heart attack and now required a bypass operation.

In the interim Sanchia had been fostered out, which had utterly terrified Gemma. She had barely been able to sleep, let alone eat. She had been desperately afraid that once the authorities had Sanchia in their grasp, she would never get her back, that no matter how much evidence she supplied to prove that she was a good mother, she would lose her baby girl.

Luckily, Lauren, who had a houseful of kids, had managed to convince the welfare caseworker to release Sanchia into her care until Gemma could get back into the country. Although Lauren had stressed to Gemma that it was a one-off favor and the situation couldn't go on for too long. With four children of her own, she was ultrabusy and on a shoestring budget.

Gemma had broken into her savings and transferred a chunk of money to Lauren, but there was no getting past the fact that she was out of luck, and almost out of time.

After all of these years of struggling as a solo parent, she was on the verge of losing her baby. She now had one imperative, and one only: to convince the welfare agency that she *was* a suitable mother for Sanchia. After racking her brains for days, she kept coming back to a desperate but foolproof solution. If she could establish that she was in a relationship with a view to marriage, that would instantly provide the stability they wanted.

Her only believable hope for marriage was her ex-boss, who she had dated for the past couple of years. Despite being a bachelor with a wild reputation, Zane fulfilled a lot of the qualities on her personal wish list for a husband. He was gorgeous, honorable and likable, and most of all, he loved kids. She had often thought that when she was ready to fall in love again, it should be with Zane.

He also happened to be the man whom the tabloids had claimed she'd had a series of on-again, off-again affairs with. It wasn't true; so far they really were just friends, but it was also a fact that whenever Zane had needed a date for a business or charity function, he had consistently come back to her.

For a man who was as wary of intimacy as Zane, that was significant. Gemma had poked and prodded at the issue until she was tired of thinking about it. In the end she had decided that if Zane really did nurture a secret passion then he was obviously waiting for a *sign* from her, or a situation, that would allow him to declare his feelings.

If they got engaged, in one stroke the untrue claims of both the nanny and the tabloids would be discredited. The "notorious affair" would instantly morph into a relationship and the notoriety that had been attached to Gemma would be discredited because it was a well-known fact that the tabloids sensationalized everything. The fact that Zane was currently here, on Medinos, had set the plan in concrete.

The only aspect that worried Gemma was that Zane was Gabriel's cousin. If she married Zane, that would put Sanchia into Gabriel's orbit.

The silence on the other end of the phone line was punctuated by another *squeak, squeak*. "I heard you say to Aunty Lauren you've got *someone in mind*."

The verbatim piece of conversation made Gemma frown. Smoothly ignoring Sanchia's insistence, she changed the subject and asked her about her cousins.

"The wallflower lady came to visit us today—"

The welfare lady. Gemma's heart pounded at the cut-off statement, the brief rustling sound as if someone else had taken the phone. A split second later, her sister came on the line.

"Gemma? It's okay, it was just a routine visit. She wanted to check your arrival date and luckily you had sent me your flight details, so I gave them to her."

Gemma could feel her anxiety level rising. "They didn't need to bother you. I emailed them my itinerary days ago. Plus they know the reason I'm not back in New Zealand yet is because I'm busy trying to fulfill *their* stipulation that I have a stable job."

Gemma's fingers tightened on the phone. Before everything had come to pieces she had accepted an appointment as a PA on Medinos to the Atraeus Resort's manager. She had hoped that by coming to Medinos, the Atraeus Group's head office, instead of resigning over the phone, she might be able to arrange a transfer to one of the Atraeus enterprises in New Zealand.

There was a small awkward silence. "Maybe whoever received the details didn't pass it on. You know what government departments can be like…."

Gemma took a long, deep breath and forced herself to sound light and breezy, as if it didn't matter that the welfare case worker was sneaking around, checking up on her. *Trying to take Sanchia.* "Sorry, you're absolutely right. I'm just a bit stressed."

"Don't worry." Lauren's voice was crisp. "No way will I let them take Sanchia again. Just get back soon."

"I will." No pressure.

Once she had gotten the dad.

Gemma hung up. Collecting the trolley, she made her way to the service elevator and stabbed the call button. The stainless-steel doors threw her image back at her as she waited, the shapeless smock that swamped her slim frame, cheeks now flushed, dark eyes overly bright.

She frowned. The emotion that kept clutching at her chest, her heart, was understandable. She missed Sanchia and she was ultrastressed about having to prove she was a good, stable parent. Plus it had been a shock to run into Luisa Messena and find herself plunged into the past. Into the other area in which she had been deemed not good enough.

Grimly, she switched her thoughts back to her small daughter. With her straight black hair and sparkling dark eyes, Sanchia was a touchstone she desperately needed right at that moment.

Gemma might have made mistakes, and as a single

mother she'd had to make a lot of sacrifices, but everything she had gone through had been worth it. Sanchia was the sweetest, most adorable thing in her life.

Although she was now far from being a baby. Like most of the O'Neills she had been born precocious, and she had grown up fast. The only difference was that unlike her red-haired cousins, Sanchia was dark and distinctly exotic. Just like her father.

The doors slid open. Blanking out that last thought, Gemma stepped inside and hit the ground-floor button.

Gabriel was going to marry.

She frowned, wishing she could stop her overtired brain from going in circles. The news shouldn't have meant anything to her. Years had passed; she was over the wild schoolgirl crush that had dominated her teens.

Drawing a deep breath, she tried to make an honest examination of her feelings. Dismay, old hurt and the one she didn't want to go near. The thought that somewhere, beneath all the layers of common sense and determined positive thinking, she might still harbor a few unresolved feelings for Gabriel.

Chest tight, she tried to distract herself from that possibility by watching floor numbers flash by. When that didn't work, she took a deep breath and squeezed her eyes closed for long seconds, trying to neutralize the emotion that had sneaked up on her.

Despite her efforts hot moisture leaked out from beneath her lids. It was stress and tiredness, nothing more. Using her fingers, she carefully wiped her cheeks, careful not to smear her mascara.

The doors slid open onto an empty corridor. Relieved, Gemma pushed the trolley into the service area and left it near the door to the kitchens. Head now throbbing with a definite headache, she walked to the sleek office that should have been officially hers as of next week, if the child welfare authorities hadn't changed her priorities.

Instead of settling in her new job on Medinos and bringing Sanchia over to live with her here, she was now flying home on the first available flight. This office, and the job she had been about to start, would now be someone else's.

Collecting the resignation she had written earlier, she walked briskly through to the manager's office. It was empty, which was a relief, and she just placed it on his blotter. He was probably personally conducting other VIP guests, all here to attend the launch party of Ambrosi Pearls the following evening, to their rooms.

With her resignation now official, Gemma felt, if not relieved, at least a sense of closure.

As she turned to leave, she noticed a typed guest list for the Ambrosi Pearls party. It was being held at the Castello Atraeus, but resort personnel and chefs were handling the catering.

She flipped the list around. Gabriel Messena's name leaped out at her.

She felt as if all the breath had just been knocked from her lungs. He would be here, on Medinos, tomorrow night.

An odd feeling of inevitability, a dizzying sense of déjà vu, hit her, which was crazy. With an effort of will, she dismissed the notion that fate was somehow throwing them back together.

Gabriel appearing on the scene right now, when she was trying to cope with a long-distance custody battle for Sanchia, was sheer coincidence. He was about to get engaged. There was no way on this earth she should ask for his assistance despite the fact that he was Sanchia's biological father.

She needed to stick to her plan.

If Zane truly did want her, and they could cement their

relationship in some public way, all of her problems would be solved. The welfare people could no longer claim she was an irresponsible "good-time girl," the nanny's lies would be discredited and her financial situation would no longer be a problem.

Although, scarily, to get them to that point, she was going to have to take the initiative and somehow jolt them off the platonic plateau they had been stranded on for the past two years.

It was possible that Zane felt constrained by the fact that she worked for his family company. But as of today, she was a free agent. The specter of an employer/employee relationship was no longer an issue.

Three

Gabriel checked his wristwatch as he walked off his flight to Medinos and into the first-class lounge, which was filled with a number of businessmen and groups of gaudily dressed tourists.

Impatiently, he skimmed the occupants. His younger brother, Nick, who was due in from a flight from Dubai, had requested an urgent meeting with him here.

Five minutes and half a cup of dark espresso later, Gabriel glanced up as Nick strolled in, looking broad-shouldered and relaxed in a dark polo and trousers. Dropping into the seat next to Gabriel, he flipped his briefcase open.

Gabriel took the thick document Nick handed him, a building contract for a high-rise in Sydney, a thick sheaf of plans and a set of costings. "Good flight?"

Nick grunted and gave him a "you've got to be kidding" look, then transferred his attention to the newspaper Gabriel had set down on the coffee table with its glaringly bright photograph. "Zane." Amused exasperation lightened his expression. "In the news again, with another woman."

For reasons he didn't want to examine, Gabriel folded the newspaper and placed it on the floor beside his briefcase.

He had read the article again on the flight. The journalist hadn't gone so far as to say the child was Zane's—the details supplied had been sketchy and inflammatory—but the inference was clear enough.

Turning his attention back to the document Nick wanted him to look over, he forced himself to concentrate on his family's most pressing problem. An archaic clause in his father's will, and his elderly uncle and trustee, Mario Atraeus, which together had the power to bankrupt them all if he didn't move swiftly.

The situation had been workable until Mario had started behaving erratically, refusing to sign crucial documents and "losing" others. Holdups and glitches were beginning to hamper the bank's ability to meet its financial obligations.

Lately, Mario's eccentricities had escalated another notch, when he had tried to use his power as trustee to leverage a marriage between Gabriel and Mario's adopted daughter, Eva Atraeus.

In that moment, Gabriel had understood what lay behind Mario's machinations. A widower, he was worried about dying and leaving his adoptive daughter alone and unmarried. In his mind, steeped in Medinian traditions, he would not have done his job as a father if he hadn't assured a good marriage for Eva.

Gabriel, as the unmarried head of the Messena family, had become Mario's prime matchmaking target.

Gabriel was clear on one point, however. When he finally got around to choosing a wife, it would be a matter of his choice, not Mario's, or anyone else's.

He would not endure a marriage of convenience simply to honor family responsibilities.

Placing the document on the coffee table, he checked his watch. "I can't release the funds. I wish I could. I'll have to run it past Mario."

A muscle pulsed along the side of Nick's jaw. "It took him two months to approve the last payment. If I renege now, the building contractor will walk."

"Leave it with me. I'll be able to swing something. Or Mario might sign."

"There is one solution. You could get married." Nick's expression was open and ingenuous as he referred to the grace clause in their father's will, which had its base in Medinian tradition. Namely, that a formally engaged or a married man was more responsible and committed than a single one. It was the one loophole that would decisively end Mario's trusteeship of his father's will and place control of the company securely in Gabriel's hands.

Nick slipped his cell out of his briefcase. "Or you could get engaged. An engagement can be easily terminated."

Gabriel sent his younger brother a frowning glance, which was wasted as Nick was busy reactivating the phone and flicking through messages. No doubt organizing his own very busy, very crowded, private life.

Sometimes he wondered if any of his five brothers and sisters even registered the fact that he was male, single and possessed a private life of his own, even if it was echoingly empty. "There won't be a marriage, or an engagement. There's a simpler solution. A psychological report on Mario would provide the grounds we need to end his trusteeship."

Either that, or hope that he could work around the financial restraints Mario was applying for another tortuous six months until he turned thirty-one and could legally take full control of the family firm.

"Good luck with getting Uncle Mario to a doctor." Nick's gaze was glued to the screen of his cell as he thumbed in a text message. "I don't know how you stay so calm."

By never allowing himself to get emotionally involved with his own family.

The practice kept him isolated and a little lonely, but at least he stayed sane.

Nick gave up texting and sat back on the couch, the good-humored distraction replaced by a frown. "Mario could ruin us, you know. If you can get him to the doctor, how long will it take to get the report?"

Gabriel repressed his irritation that Nick didn't seem to get it that the last thing Mario wanted to do at this juncture was cooperate in the process of proving that he was past it, and wresting his power from him. "I'm seeing Mario as soon as I get back from Medinos."

Nick rolled his eyes. "Before or after his nap?"

Gabriel crumpled his empty foam cup and tossed it into a nearby trash can. "Probably during."

Nick said something short and flat. "If I can't get the family firm to finance me, I will go elsewhere."

Otherwise he would lose his shirt financially. Their younger brother, Damian, was in the same position, as were a number of key clients. If Gabriel couldn't streamline their process, they could lose a lot of business. Worst-case scenario, the bank's financial rating would be downgraded and they would lose a whole lot more.

Gabriel checked his wristwatch, placed the document in his briefcase, collected the newspaper and rose to his feet.

Nick followed suit, picking up his briefcase. "My finance deadline is one week. I don't want to take my business elsewhere."

"With any luck, you won't have to. Apparently Constantine wants a favor." His cousin Constantine Atraeus was the whole reason Gabriel was on Medinos in the first place. Constantine, who was the head of the Atraeus Group and enormously wealthy, was sympathetic about Gabriel's situation. He had faced a similar problem with his own father, Lorenzo, Mario's brother, who had behaved just as erratically in his old age.

Nick grinned. "Cool, that means you've got leverage."

But Gabriel didn't miss the flat note in Nick's voice. If he couldn't obtain Constantine's backing to have Mario removed as trustee, and at the same time extend Gabriel a personal line of credit that Mario couldn't interfere with, Nick would walk.

His brother kept pace with him as he strode toward his gate. He directed a frowning glance at the folded paper. "Isn't the girl with Zane the O'Neill girl from Dolphin Bay you dated once?"

Gabriel's jaw tightened. He hadn't expected Nick to remember Gemma. "It wasn't exactly a date."

Date was the last word he would use to describe the unscripted, passionate night they had spent together in a deserted beach house. "Gemma works for the Atraeus Group. She was Zane's PA."

Nick shrugged. "That explains it, then. You know what the tabloids are like. They were probably just out on some business date."

"Maybe." But if the child was Zane's, there was no question that Gemma had gotten herself entangled with Zane, to her detriment.

And if that was the case then he bore some of the responsibility for her predicament. If Gabriel hadn't been in

Sydney the day the Atraeus Group was interviewing for office staff and put in a glowing recommendation, Gemma would never have beaten off some of the applicants who had applied for the position.

Unwittingly, Gabriel's recommendation had eventually put Gemma directly in Zane's path.

He didn't know Zane as well as he knew his other two Atraeus cousins, Lucas and Constantine, but well enough to know that marriage had never been Zane's favorite topic. He was more interested in short flings.

Or, apparently, longer, convenient arrangements.

Something snapped in him at the thought that Gemma had allowed herself to be seduced into a liaison with his cousin when Zane's interest was self-serving and superficial. Despite the child, marriage obviously wasn't on his agenda.

As he approached the exit doors for the airport, he recalled one other piece of information the article had offered. Apparently Gemma had just made the move from Sydney to Medinos in order to be close to Zane.

The fact that Gemma had been left out on a limb with a child, but was still intent on maintaining some kind of relationship with Zane shouldn't matter to him, but it did.

The decision to reclaim Gemma settled in. If Zane had shown any hint that he wanted to commit, Gabriel would have backed off, but he hadn't. Zane seemed quite happy to allow Gemma to shoulder all of the responsibility for the child. Added to that, Gabriel had made some private inquiries during the stopover in Dubai and discovered that Zane had been seeing someone else.

As far as Gabriel was concerned that settled the matter. Gemma was vulnerable and in need of rescue and he planned on being her rescuer.

He didn't know how or when the opportunity would

arise; all he knew was that with Zane's cavalier attitude and a new girlfriend in the mix, it would be sooner rather than later.

Gemma mingled with the guests at the Ambrosi Pearls party, to which she had gained entry by using the invitation she had received a couple of days earlier.

Accepting a flute of champagne from a waiter, she skimmed the crowded reception room of the Castello Atraeus, which was lit by the soft shimmer of chandeliers. Elegant groupings of candles and bouquets of white roses and glossy dark greenery added a hothouse glamour to the room, which suddenly seemed to be filled with tall, dark lions of men. Wealthy and powerful members of both the Atraeus and Messena families.

Gemma's heart skipped a beat as she caught a glimpse of broad, sleek shoulders, a clean, masculine profile and tough jaw. Even though she had come prepared for a face-to-face meeting with Gabriel, for a split second her heart seemed to stop in her chest.

The glittering crowd of guests shifted, a kaleidoscopic array of expensive jewelry and designer gowns, affording her an even clearer view.

In the wash of light from a chandelier, Gabriel's features were tanned, as if he'd spent time outside under a hot sun, his jaw rock solid and darkened by the shadow of stubble. His hair, gleaming and coal-black, was longer than she remembered, now brushing the collar of his shirt.

Her fingers tightened on the lace clutch that matched her simple but elegant black dress.

Realizing just how tight her nerves were strung, Gemma reminded herself to breathe. She had hoped against hope that Gabriel wouldn't actually attend the party. He didn't normally show up at lavish promotional parties, even though he was often invited. On the few previous occasions that he had actually attended, she had usually found out ahead of time and found an excuse not to be there. Tonight she didn't have that option. In order to buttonhole Zane, it was an absolute imperative that she was here.

A group of beautifully dressed women obscured her view, then she caught sight of Gabriel again. In that moment, as if drawn by her intensity, his head turned and the dark gaze that had continued to haunt one too many of Gemma's dreams locked on hers.

Her heart slammed in her chest. Any idea that Gabriel hadn't known she was here dissolved. He had, and from the way his brows jerked together, he wasn't pleased to see her.

A sharp little pang of hurt shocked her into immobility.

Taking a steadying breath, Gemma did her best to shake off her oversensitive reaction. Unnerved by the direct eye contact, she placed her half-full champagne flute on a side table. Neatly changing direction, she almost walked into a waiter with a loaded tray.

Blushing and mumbling an apology, she sidestepped the waiter and threaded her way through the suddenly overheated, overperfumed room. A little desperately she noted that there was still no sign of Zane, who she was hoping would have been here early so she could get this whole situation resolved one way or another.

As she walked she was unbearably aware that, even though she could no longer see Gabriel, he was still watching her.

Her stomach clenched on an uncharacteristic burst of panic.

She had known Gabriel could attend, so it shouldn't have been such a shock to see him. She just wished that her perfect record of avoidance hadn't ended tonight of all nights.

A knot of guests parted and Zane finally appeared, striding directly toward her.

Nerves strung almost to breaking point, she noted the three studs in Zane's lobe, which she had always privately thought were a little over the top, unlike Gabriel's sleek tailored suit, which conferred a quiet, rock-solid power.

Calling on all of her acting skills, she tried to project her usual bright, outgoing persona.

The quick hug, which was punctuated by the intrusive flash of a camera, was not unusual between friends, but in that moment, hugging Zane felt horribly fake.

She was the problem, Gemma realized. Until she had seen Gabriel, her decision to try to shift her dating friendship with Zane into a regular relationship and enlist his help in getting Sanchia back had seemed viable. Now, in the space of just a couple of minutes, everything had changed.

Seeing Gabriel had unnerved her in ways she couldn't have imagined. One piercing look from him and she felt guilty about choosing Zane, as if in some subtle way she was betraying Gabriel, which was ridiculous. While it was true he was Sanchia's biological father, that was all he ever had been, or could be.

It was a relief when Zane, who appeared as distracted as she, didn't respond in a positive way to her labored attempt to catapult their friendship into more intimate territory or show any desire to linger.

When he turned down her suggestion that they should go out onto the terrace, so she could launch into the very private conversation she needed to have with him, unnerved, Gemma made for the nearest exit. As she hurried out, her spine tingled with the knowledge that Gabriel was in the room and that he had witnessed her hugging Zane.

In that moment she saw her actions from Gabriel's viewpoint and she didn't like the needy picture that formed.

Anger stiffened her spine. For the first time in her life she was attempting to lose the strong independent streak that had been ingrained from childhood and ask a man she liked if he would consider having a relationship with her.

Gabriel could disapprove all he liked, but it was a fact that he had stepped out of the picture six years ago.

Plan A had failed. Now, unfortunately, she would have to resort to Plan B.

Four

Gabriel refused the glass of champagne a waiter offered him. His dark gaze swept the crowded reception room. A knot of gray-suited Japanese businessmen shifted and he was rewarded with another clear view of creamy skin, flame hair and black lace.

Constantine Atraeus lifted a brow. "Gemma O'Neill. Girl's going places, or was. She's just had to resign, a personal commitment."

An instant replay of Gemma stepping into Zane's arms made his jaw tighten. Then Constantine's statement about Gemma resigning because of a personal commitment sank in.

His gaze sliced back to Constantine, with whom he'd been closeted earlier in the day, during which time he had agreed to oversee the start-up of a new Ambrosi Pearls venture in Auckland. However, he'd been unable to commit to a loan from the Atraeus Group because Mario was a significant shareholder and would instantly veto the deal. He could raise the amount Gabriel needed personally, but it would take time, which Gabriel currently didn't have. "She's finally gotten engaged to Zane?"

"Zane?" Constantine looked surprised. "As far as I know they're friends, and that's all. It's not public yet, but Zane is on the verge of getting engaged to Lilah Cole. Although, an engagement is probably exactly what Gemma needs at this point."

Gabriel frowned at Constantine's reference to another tabloid story he had found online, that Gemma was having custody difficulties with her small daughter.

Constantine's wife, Sienna, a gorgeous blonde, joined them, ending the conversation. The next time Gabriel searched out Gemma, she had disappeared from sight, and so had Zane. Jaw tight, he excused himself and went outside.

The large stone terrace, with its spectacular view across a deceptively smooth stretch of sea to the island of Ambrus and the clear, star-studded sky, was empty. The tension that hummed through him loosened off a notch. Walking to the parapet, he gripped the railing and stared at the line of luminescence on the far horizon, the last soft glimmer of the setting sun.

He didn't know what he would have done if he had found Gemma and Zane locked in an intimate clinch. His reaction to the situation so far had not been either considered or tactical, it had simply been knee-jerk.

Gaze still caught and held by the purity of sky and sea, he let the soft chill of the night settle around him. An image from the past, of dark red hair across his chest, Gemma soft and warm against him, filled his mind, blotting out the night sky.

In the midst of the grief and betrayal of his father's

death there had been no time for the passion that had hit him like a thunderbolt.

But that was six years ago. Since then the situation had changed. His family had recovered from the double blow of his father's death and the resulting scandal. The bank's financial performance had been brilliant, thanks to his careful management and his younger brother, Kyle's, flare for investment. The only fly in the ointment was Mario and his machinations, which had recently begun to stall business.

The raw relief he'd experienced when Constantine had said Zane was about to get engaged to Lilah Cole, a high-profile designer for Ambrosi Pearls, replayed itself.

His fingers tightened on the parapet as he recalled the earlier sight of Gemma with her arms around Zane's neck. It was clear that she didn't understand she had lost Zane to another woman.

The fact that Zane hadn't had the courage to inform Gemma he was going to marry someone else made his jaw tighten. If he wasn't mistaken, Gemma was about to be badly hurt.

It wasn't exactly a repeat of the situation that had thrown them together six years ago, but it was oddly close.

The thought that, after years of careful control, utter focus on his work and family life, he could step into the maelstrom of passion that had swept him away in Dolphin Bay tightened every muscle in his body, but the desire to do so was tempered with caution. He couldn't forget the power of the obsessive passion that had ensnared his father. There was no way he could abandon himself to desire, and suddenly he had his plan.

Gemma needed relationship stability in order to establish custody of her child. With Constantine unable to guarantee the loan he needed within a forty-eight-hour framework, he could use a believable fiancée, on a strictly temporary basis, to cut through the legal clauses preventing him from taking full control of his company.

A fake engagement would provide the solutions they both needed and in his case, a safe, controlled environment in which to explore the passion that coursed through his veins.

Satisfied, he left the terrace and strolled back into the Castello and the ornate reception room. Gemma was nowhere to be seen. Neither was Zane.

He would find Gemma, it was just a matter of time. Thanks to boyhood holidays spent running wild on Medinos, he knew every nook and cranny of the Castello. He only hoped he didn't find Zane with her. If that was the case, he decided coldly, he would deal with the situation in the time-honored way, down on the beach and without an audience.

Gemma walked quickly down a small corridor and stepped into an anteroom that was currently used to hold coats and wraps. Closing the door behind her, she leaned on it for long seconds, allowing her breathing and her heart rate to steady.

Pushing away from the cold, dark wood of the door, she searched amongst the jumble of bags to find the canvas bag she had stashed in the room earlier.

Relief flooded her as her fingers closed over the strap. Hauling it from out of the expensive collection of designer handbags, she placed it on an ornate carved table that had probably been in existence for centuries and was no doubt worth an obscene amount of money.

The fact that the Atraeus family could put an heirloom antique in a room that was little more than a storage room underlined the yawning abyss between their lives and hers. Zane was not a typical Atraeus, which was another reason why she had found him so easy to get on with. Even though he bore the name Atraeus, he hadn't come from wealth originally. He understood what it was like to be poor.

Fingers shaking with an overload of adrenaline, she checked the black lace negligee and a bottle of champagne that was rapidly losing its chill. At the bottom of the bag she had also stowed a glossy magazine she'd found with an article titled "How To Seduce Your Man in Ten Easy Ways."

After careful thought, she had chosen the birthday surprise scenario, with her as the surprise. Nervous terror clutched at her just at the thought of actually having to resort to that tactic. Even viewing it as a scene she was acting, she wasn't sure she could go through with it.

At the last minute, she had also slipped into her evening bag an envelope of melt-your-heart snapshots of Sanchia.

Plan C. Just in case she couldn't go through with the seduction plan.

Gemma hurried down a corridor lined with cold fortress stone and archaic-looking brass lamps that glowed a soft buttery gold in the dimness. Mouth dry, she opened the door to Zane's private quarters, using the spare key she had obtained from the cleaner's office downstairs, and stepped inside.

A large sitting room with French doors opened onto a stone terrace. An ultramodern kitchenette occupied an alcove. Opening the fridge, she placed the now warm bottle of French champagne on a shelf to chill.

Briskly, she set about completing her preparations. If Zane had only agreed to talk to her, she wouldn't have had to resort to these lengths, but as she stepped into Zane's bedroom and was confronted with what looked like a king-size bed, the risk she was taking suddenly loomed large.

A niggling doubt surfaced. Encountering Zane's coolness at the launch party had leached away her confidence. The fear that she had resolutely suppressed, that proposing a real relationship was a ludicrous solution, came back to haunt her.

The idea of proposing a fake engagement was seeming more and more viable.

The fact that she had an alternative solution cheered her up and brought her normal positivity and optimism bouncing back to the surface.

Heart beating even faster, she walked through to the bedroom, her gaze automatically flinching from the king-size bed.

Now that it had come to the crunch, her seduction plan seemed basically unworkable because of one chilly little fact. Sexually, so far, she hadn't really felt anything for Zane.

It was a glitch she had happily glossed over, but that now loomed large—a fatal flaw in her plan.

She didn't know why she couldn't quite whip up the enthusiasm to fall passionately in love with Zane, despite both working and socializing with him. According to magazines and tabloids, practically every other woman on the planet was desperate for her ex-boss.

Instead she was shaking like a leaf and suddenly the whole idea of touching Zane, of actually shifting out of the comfortable casual friendship they'd shared to actually kissing him, seemed absurd.

An image of Gabriel and his cool, assessing gaze flashed into her mind. She stopped dead in the middle of the high-ceilinged lounge decorated in the spare but dramatic Medinian way, with dark furniture and jewel-bright Kilims scattered on the floor, her already shaky resolve wavering further. In that instant an oil painting featuring a woman draped in vivid, hot pink silk caught her eye. Pink was Sanchia's favorite color.

The thought of her daughter and their predicament was a timely reminder.

Grabbing the bag with the negligee, she walked resolutely through to the bathroom. Keeping her gaze averted from a wall-length mirror in a heavily carved gold frame, another exotic museum piece, she quickly changed into the negligee.

As she straightened and shoved her dress into the bag she caught a full frontal view of herself and blushed. With her hair tousled, her eyes dark, her pale skin gleaming through the lace, she looked like a high-priced courtesan.

That was the whole idea, of course, so she could hopefully shock Zane into seeing her as a woman instead of just a friend. But crazily, she still felt as if what she was planning was some kind of betrayal of Gabriel.

Although why should she feel guilty that after two years of dating she was finally attempting to launch her relationship with Zane on to a proper, intimate footing?

Unless, in her heart of hearts, she did still carry a torch for Gabriel?

She blinked at the thought, which had been at the edge of her mind ever since she had overheard the conversation in Gabriel's mother's hotel suite.

It would explain her emotional reaction, then the tension that had zinged through her when she had caught sight of Gabriel tonight. Not just tension that he was in the room and could possibly find out about Sanchia, but an acute feminine reaction that had shivered along her nerve endings and heightened all of her senses.

The kind of reaction that had hit her six years ago, and that had ended in a pregnancy.

The kind of reaction she had failed to feel for Zane.

The stark realization that she had been incapable of falling for anyone since the passionate interlude with Gabriel hit her with enough force that she froze in place.

She drew a shaky breath, feeling faintly ill. It was time to take her head out of the sand. The utter lack of sex and passion in her life wasn't because she was too busy as a working mother, and simply too tired to date. Or that she was ultrapicky about a man's qualities because, first and foremost, she needed to choose someone who would be good for Sanchia.

It was because somehow Gabriel Messena did still matter to her in a deep, intimate, personal way.

Blankly, she walked out of the bathroom. Stomach tight, legs feeling like noodles, she came to a halt in the middle of the sitting room. Dazed, she stared at the cool white walls, the rich trappings of the room. She didn't know how it could have happened, just that it had.

On an intellectual level, she had convinced herself that she had cut ties with Gabriel and wasn't attracted to him in any way. But the problem was that she had been a virgin when they had made love. Gabriel was her first and only lover. She had never fallen for anyone else in her entire life, including her teenage years. All of her experiences of love, sex and passion were bound up with Gabriel.

It was no wonder her body had reacted. She had seen Gabriel and the emotions and sensations she had only ever experienced with him, and that she had never gotten closure for, had resurfaced.

A knock on the door sent adrenaline shooting through her veins.

Logic told her it couldn't be Zane; he wouldn't knock. The thought that it could be Gabriel made the breath catch in her throat, although the whole idea that, after glimpsing her at the party, he would come after her, or even know that she was in Zane's room, was ridiculous. He hadn't contacted her in years, so why would he now?

Clutching the lapels of her negligee together, she gripped the medieval iron door handle and opened the door a crack. It was Lilah. Knowledge and guilt seared her as she registered the hurt in the other woman's gaze.

She had known Lilah was attracted to Zane and seemed to be pursuing him with limited success. She had ignored the complication, because a great many women had chased after Zane.

Lilah's expression chilled as she took in what Gemma was wearing. "You should stop trying and go home. Sex won't make Zane, or any man, have a relationship with you."

A sharp pain stabbed at her heart. Six years ago, instead of bringing them closer together, sex had destroyed any chance of a relationship with Gabriel. He had probably thought that she always gave in on a first date.

Although why she was thinking about Gabriel again, when this situation was entirely different, she didn't know. The whole point of the seduction scenario was that Zane would see her as the woman she was and stop treating her like a younger sister.

She lifted her chin. "How can you know that?"

The same pain Gemma had experienced just seconds ago flashed in the other woman's gaze. With a jolt, Gemma realized that Lilah was in love with Zane.

"Logic. If you couldn't make him fall in love with you in two years, then it's probably not going to happen."

The fatal flaw in her plan.

Relief rolled through Gemma. Lilah had stated the one simple fact that she had somehow managed to talk herself around, but that happily undermined every one of her plans. Time had passed and nothing had happened between her and Zane, and there had been plenty of opportunities.

She had put it down to the fact that she was always so tired and stressed with juggling Sanchia, a never-ending stream of nannies and a job that often included travel. Sex had just not been a priority. But it should have been for a hot alpha male like Zane.

The grim fact was that they were more like brother and sister than possible lovers.

Sudden embarrassed heat washed through her as she realized how exposed she was to Lilah, dressed for seduction and obviously waiting for Zane. And now she couldn't wait to leave.

Zane. Panic jolted through her.

She had to get out of his suite before he found her.

With a brief apologetic look toward Lilah, she closed the door, found the bag with her dress and raced to the bathroom. Wrenching the negligee off, not caring when the fine silk and lace caught and tore, she fumbled into her dress, dragged the zipper up and jammed the negligee into the bag, out of sight.

She did a quick check of the bathroom and bedroom to make sure she left nothing behind. Walking through to the small kitchenette, she retrieved the bottle of champagne she had put in the fridge.

Embarrassed heat burned her cheeks as she found her shoes, jammed them on her feet and did a last hurried check of the sitting room before she left.

She must have been mad, certifiable, in thinking that she could have convinced Zane Atraeus that she could be more than just an employee and friend, that she could possibly be his lover or his wife. It was the same mad optimism she had clutched at when she had made the mistake of sleeping with Gabriel.

She could still remember the dull depression when she had realized that the few hours they had spent together hadn't meant a thing to him, and she'd heard the relief in his voice when she'd said she wasn't pregnant.

Lilah Cole's pale, blank expression minutes ago said it all. Gorgeous, hot billionaires did not marry small-town girls with no substance behind them. Slinging the strap of her evening bag over her shoulder, she headed for the door, now desperate to get out of the suite. But as she reached for the handle, Murphy's law—the one that states that what can go wrong, will go wrong—kicked in. The door popped open and Zane strode in.

An excruciating few moments later, after realizing a stunning truth, that Zane was in love with Lilah, Gemma made a hasty escape.

A giddy sense of relief clutched at her as she practically jogged down the corridor. High heels tapping on flag-stones, she almost failed to recognize a reporter she had seen circulating at the party walking straight toward her.

She caught his sly grin as she spun on her heel and started back the way she had come. She had no intention of reentering Zane's suite. There were a number of other doors, and what looked like an exit onto a terrace ahead. She would find a door, any door that was unlocked, and hide out for a few minutes.

With dismay, she noticed Zane's door, which she had closed behind her, was now ajar. A flash of movement confirmed that Zane was near the door, zipping a bag closed, on the point of leaving.

Panic clutched at her. When Zane stepped out into the corridor, the reporter would get a picture of the two of them together. Now that there was no possibility of a relationship, that was something she absolutely did not want to happen.

She broke into a jog again, determined to get past Zane's

door before he stepped out. At that moment another door popped open right in front of her. It was one of two concealed doors, which she vaguely remembered reading about when she'd studied up on the Castello, that led to the old armory and the stables. A secret network built into the fortress in case of attack, and as such designed to be unobtrusive.

A dark, masculine head ducked under the low lintel.

Startled, Gemma almost ran full tilt into him. Lean hands closed around her arms, steadying her as she clutched at broad shoulders. Heat and a clean, male scent engulfed her.

Not a member of the staff using the convenient shortcut with fresh linen or a tray, but a bona fide member of the Atraeus family who, in centuries past, would have fitted the mold of fortress protector. Gabriel Messena.

Her heart slammed against her chest at the sheer shock of running into Gabriel. The pressure of his hands on her bare skin sent a raw shiver up her spine. Almost in the same moment she registered the flash of a camera, the shadowy shape of the reporter still lurking at one end of the corridor.

Gabriel's gaze dropped to the bag she was clutching, the incriminating trail of black lace and the foil top of the champagne bottle. Knowledge flared in his dark gaze.

Hot color washed across her skin, her stomach clenched on an acid burn of shame. She didn't know how, but Gabriel knew exactly what she had attempted.

Instead of loosening his hold, his fingers tightened, anchoring her in place, close enough that she could feel the heat radiating from his big body.

His head bent, his breath feathered her cheek, warm and damp. "Zane is about to get engaged." The sexy low timbre of his voice shivered all the way to her toes, making places inside her that should be frozen and immune instantly melt. "If you don't want the newspapers to report that you've moved from being Zane's girlfriend to his mistress, you should consider kissing me."

Five

Another flash from the reporter's camera lit up the dim corridor, making her stomach hollow out. Although not as much as the knowledge that Gabriel must have read the various tabloid stories and assumed that she was involved in an affair with Zane. "I know Zane wants Lilah. *Now*."

Something like relief registered in his gaze. "Good."

Her jaw tightened against another heated rush of humiliation. In terms of the welfare case against her, she absolutely could not afford to be viewed as Zane Atraeus's mistress. "One kiss."

Lifting up on her toes, she braced her palms on the hard muscle of his shoulders. The firm touch of his hands at her waist, drawing her closer, sent a sensual shock through her as she took a shallow breath and touched her mouth to his.

The kiss, as brief as it was, sent sensation shivering through her, unexpectedly powerful and laced with memories that were still sharp-edged and bittersweet.

The humid warmth of a summer's night, the sibilant wash of waves on the beach, the weight of Gabriel's body pressing down on hers...

She inhaled and the faintly resinous scent of his cologne shivered through her. If she hadn't known before that she had made a mistake in kissing Gabriel, she knew it then.

It had taken her years to be able to view what they had shared as a casual encounter that had gotten out of hand, years to get over his easy defection.

The heated tension cut off as another camera flash temporarily blinded her, followed by the sound of retreating footsteps as the reporter made his escape.

The reporter. Her stomach churned at the new publicity, which she hated, even though she knew that in this case kissing Gabriel had been expedient. Doing so negated the earlier, potentially damning photo that had been taken of her hugging Zane.

Gabriel's head lifted, and in that instant she was aware of the creak of a door opening a few meters down the hall. It was Zane. Thankfully, his back was to her as he stepped out into the corridor, juggling bags and keys.

A split second later, darkness engulfed her as Gabriel pulled her through the opening into the narrow space behind the wall and even more tightly into his arms.

The door, which appeared to be spring-loaded, snicked shut behind her, the fit seamless, closing them into a dim, claustrophobic hallway that smelled of damp and ages-old dust. She had expected the ancient hide to be pitch-black, but surprisingly, the very modern glow of an electric lightbulb glowed at one end, illuminating a stone stairwell.

Heart still pounding with an overload of adrenaline and the curious humming excitement of being close to Gabriel, she released herself from his hold and stepped back in the narrow space. Her bare back brushed against smooth stone, cool enough to make her flinch.

Closeted in the narrow space, with the pressure of his kiss still tingling on her mouth, it felt, crazily enough, as if they were a couple. For a few dizzying seconds Gemma ceased to think about everything that had gone wrong and simply wallowed in the moment.

"This way." Gabriel indicated the set of stone steps ahead. "They go down to the armory and the stables, which have both been converted into garages and a guest suite. Not exactly as romantic as the old days, but a convenient shortcut if you've forgotten your car keys."

She caught the flash of his grin and out of nowhere her stomach turned a somersault.

The small warning jolt that went with that reaction was swamped by a surge of pure happiness as she found herself smiling back. She had just done a completely stupid thing: she had embarrassed and humiliated herself with the bungled seduction attempt and a reporter was brewing another scandal. But as she stood, crowded close to Gabriel in the secret hideaway, a dangerous thrill shot down her spine.

Lips still damp and tingling, on edge and acutely aware of the intimacy of being alone with the one man she thought she would never be alone with again, Gemma followed Gabriel.

Her stomach churned at how close she had come to disaster. She knew why she had kissed Gabriel. It had been the rescue she had needed, but she had no idea why he had kissed her.

With every second that passed the gratitude that had flooded her when he had stepped in to help dissipated, and Gabriel's presence in the exact moment when she had needed help became stranger and more confusing. Kindness? Definitely. Desire?

She drew a sharp breath at the question that had been hovering at the back of her mind. Not seriously.

As he paused at the top of the stairwell, the light from the bare bulb gleamed over taut cheekbones, a blade-straight nose and the lash of an old scar over one temple. As his gaze locked with hers, she remembered with a small jolt that he had gotten the scar during a knife attack on Medinos when he was a teenager.

Trained in self-defence, as were all the members of his family, he had taken the knife and ended the attempted mugging, but the scar invested Gabriel with a barbaric quality. New Zealand born he may be, but she couldn't let herself forget that he was the head of an ancient and wealthy family that could trace its lineage back centuries.

"Don't worry about the reporter, he can't follow unless he knows where the mechanism that opens the door is, which reminds me…"

He paused at the head of the steps, his expression shifting instantly back to neutral as he slid his cell out of his trouser pocket.

His conversation with the Castello's security—who should have checked the man's press credentials—was brief and to the point. His gaze touched on hers again as he hung up. "I didn't see a press card on his lapel. If he doesn't have an invitation, with any luck, they'll stop him before he gets out of the Castello and erase the pictures."

Her face burning uncomfortably hot again, Gemma glanced down at the incriminating gleam of black lace in the carry bag, the handle of which was still looped over one arm. Surreptitiously, she tucked the negligee lower. "Thank you."

Although she didn't hold out much hope that erasing the photos from the reporter's camera would be the end of the matter. Knowing her luck, the photos had already been emailed to the editor of some tabloid scandal sheet.

"When we reach ground level, we'll be close to where my car is parked. If you want I can give you a ride back to your hotel."

Gemma sent him another strained smile. "You don't have to do that." She already felt stressed and indebted to Gabriel. Now that she was finally back to thinking logically, rather than simply panicking and reacting, the last thing she wanted was to impose on him any further. "I've got my cell with me. I can call a taxi."

Pausing beneath the glare of the single bulb, he glanced at his wristwatch. "If you haven't prebooked a taxi, you'll probably have to wait. Medinos doesn't have that many, and when Constantine throws a party, they're mostly booked in advance by the guests." His gaze touched on hers. "You could always wait out front. Chances are you could find someone who will be willing to share one with you."

A shudder of pure horror went through Gemma. In that moment, she was also certain that Gabriel knew that standing on the front steps of the Castello, where journalists could easily find her, was the absolute last thing she wanted.

That meant he had probably read the press stories about her, which made sense of his timely appearance almost directly across from Zane's suite. She was grateful he had decided to intervene, although wary of his motives. Given that he had suggested the kiss, she would be naive to discount the fact that as crazy as it seemed, Gabriel still felt something for her. As seductive as that fact was, she was also overwhelmingly aware of the danger. Gabriel had the power to make things better, but if he ever discovered that he was the father of her child, he could also cause further complications.

Lifting her chin, she met his gaze. "I think you know that exposing myself to any further media attention is not exactly at the top of my 'to do' list."

"I know there's a child. I also know there's a problem with custody, in which case pressuring Zane was the last thing you should have tried."

Gabriel watched the warm color drain from Gemma's face, leaving her looking pale and a little shocked. He hadn't meant to be so blunt, but neither did he have much patience with subtler approaches.

He vowed to have a word with Zane before he left Medinos. He didn't care how irresistible his cousin found Gemma, if he was getting engaged—in Gabriel's book— that meant that he now left Gemma alone, permanently.

A heady sense of satisfaction wound through him as he led the way down the steep flight of worn steps. Sound and light receded as they descended a good three levels and ended up in a dank and chilly hallway. Flagged with stone, the narrow corridor ran alongside the kitchens and pantries, and was redolent of the smells of a spicy Medinian fish stew and fresh-baked bread. Opening a squat, heavy door, he ducked under another low lintel and stepped out onto the windy northern side of the Castello.

A cold breeze, laden with sea salt, funnelled through the narrow alleyway that ran between the Castello and a set of garages. As he held out his hand to Gemma, her hair fluttered in the breeze. Gleaming strands flowed across his shoulder, sliding gossamer-soft against his jaw, filling his nostrils with the warm, tantalizing scent of gardenias.

She tucked stray strands behind one ear. As she did so her evening bag, which was hitched over one shoulder by a thin gold chain, slipped to the ground. Muttering beneath her breath, she set the carry bag down and bent to retrieve the delicate lace evening bag that matched her dress.

Gabriel beat her to it. As he handed the evening bag to her, he checked out the contents of the much larger bag. The glint of foil was definitely the top of a bottle of champagne, and the trailing black lace and silk was not the wrap he had hoped it would be; it was lingerie of some sort.

The quick twist of anger settled into a cold moment of decision.

With a smooth motion, he picked up the bag. "I can take this for you."

With a startled glance, Gemma reached for it. "Thanks, but that won't be necessary."

Instead of hooking the strap of the evening bag back over her shoulder, she dropped it on top of the carry bag. The action effectively concealed the lingerie and champagne, which only succeeded in firing the edgy temper he hadn't known he possessed even further.

He had no problem putting a name to the burning emotion that lately seemed to continually overpower him.

Jealousy.

Annoyed with the fierce emotion and his inability to control it, he shifted position to shield Gemma from the wind. As he did so a flash of movement drew his eye.

Zane was walking from the Castello's front entrance in the direction of the garages.

Gemma's gaze caught his. "Is there another way we can go?"

Grim satisfaction filled him that instead of chasing after Zane, Gemma was now intent on avoiding him. It was progress of a sort. "If you don't want to go back into the Castello, I can take you back to your hotel. My car is parked in the lot beside the stables, just a few meters down the path and around the corner." He jerked his head, indicating the direction.

Gemma sent him a brittle smile. "Thanks. I will take you up on that lift."

Immediately, she started down the path.

Keeping pace effortlessly, because Gemma had to negotiate the path in high heels, Gabriel glanced back in Zane's direction. Relief loosened some of his tension as he noted that his cousin had already disappeared from sight into the garage.

Common sense told him that it wasn't likely that Zane had seen them. He had been walking through a floodlit area, while they were in semidarkness.

He probably didn't need to be so cautious. But now that Gemma seemed to finally be free of Zane, he wasn't about to give his cousin the chance to change his mind and entice her back again.

As they rounded a corner, Gemma tilted her head and stared at the impressive view of the seaward-facing side of the floodlit Castello where it perched high on cliffs. Some distance below, waves dashed on rocks, filling the air with the muted background roar of surf. "This place is amazing. I would have liked to have had a proper look around—" She stopped midspeech, her expression taut. "No, cancel that. I'm over castles and wealth. I'm especially over anyone holding a camera."

Gabriel logged the sound of a powerful car, the flicker of headlights through trees as Zane accelerated down the drive. Satisfaction that his cousin was finally removed from the equation drained some of his tension. "I thought you would have visited this place a number of times."

The hollow feeling that gripped him at the thought that over the past two years Gemma would have shared

Zane's bed on frequent occasions renewed his edgy, burning tension.

Gemma sent him a startled glance. "I visited Medinos quite a lot when I was Zane's PA, but I was never invited to the Castello. This was my first, and last, visit."

Gemma halted so suddenly beneath an ancient gnarled olive tree that he almost walked into her. "What I don't get is why you're helping me?"

Because he was tired of fixing everyone else's lives and wanted his own back. Because he wanted more of what they'd shared six years ago.

An acute awareness of Gemma's nearness burned through Gabriel. The rich, tantalizing scent of gardenias teased his nostrils again. The banked anger at Zane's cavalier treatment of her flared a little hotter, and he was abruptly glad for the intense pooling darkness beneath the tree.

As soon as he had an opportunity, he intended to track Zane down and confront him with his behavior. If he was getting engaged, that meant he had established a relationship some time ago and yet had still continued to see Gemma. "Maybe I don't like the way Zane's treated you."

Surprise flickered in her gaze, and he wondered grimly what had happened to her over the past few years that she hadn't registered how shabbily she had been treated.

Her chin tilted. "Zane hasn't treated me badly. He's been extremely kind to me." Her gaze dropped to his mouth, and for a moment the air turned molten.

Drawing in a sharp breath, as if she had been just as affected as he, Gemma looked quickly away. "I like Zane. He's been a good friend. I've just had a run of bad luck, that's all."

Before he could answer, she walked briskly on ahead, and paused at a fork in the path, the sea breeze molding the black lace of her dress against her slim curves, making her look thinner than he remembered, oddly solitary and fragile.

Gabriel indicated the correct direction. His annoyance leached away as Gemma walked quickly on, now clearly wary of his presence. He had ruthlessly pushed her, moving into her personal space and suggesting the kiss. After the electrifying heat of the kiss and her unmistakable response, he had expected her to back off.

What he couldn't understand was why she was protecting Zane. The only conclusion he could draw was that despite Zane's upcoming engagement and the callous way he had dumped her, Gemma still harbored a soft spot for his cousin.

It was a complication Gabriel hadn't anticipated, and one he was determined to eradicate.

If Gemma hadn't been attracted to him, he would have stepped back from the situation, but that wasn't the case. Her response had been immediate and clear. He had seen it in the way her gaze had clung to his, the heat rimming her cheekbones, and felt it in the softness of her mouth and the rapid thud of her heart as they'd kissed.

He might have been out of the loop for a while when it came to the murky area of relationships, but one kiss and the years had spun away. He hadn't mistaken her response, and his own had been just as visceral, just as powerful, the chemistry sizzling between them hot enough to burn.

As far as he was concerned, Zane had had his chance. If he hadn't been able to commit in two years, and with a child in the mix, then he couldn't really want Gemma.

But Gabriel did.

The concept, which had grown in him over the past twenty-four hours—ever since he had read the newspaper article—was powerful and irrevocable.

Gabriel knew his nature. He was a Messena to the bone, but along with the hot-blooded, volatile streak, from an early age his father had impressed upon him the need to develop a level head and a steely discipline. As a result, when it came to the stormy seas of romance and passion, it took a great deal to sway him.

He had never been in love; he couldn't imagine the havoc that would cause, but something significant had happened between him and Gemma.

Instead of dissolving with the passage of time, the attraction had stuck with him. In six years he had been unable to forget her.

The moment was clarifying. He realized that after years of avoidance, he had finally applied the deliberate, methodical process he used to weigh a business proposition, and he had reached a moment of clear decision.

In this case it was a definite *yes* to more than just passion.

A sharp thrill shot down his spine at the thought of picking up on the relationship that had been snuffed out before it had had a chance six years ago.

He filled his lungs with tangy sea air and felt more alive than he had in years. Six years to be exact, since the last time he had experienced genuine passion, in a small, sandy beach house in Dolphin Bay.

Six

A disorienting sense of déjà vu, an odd feeling of inevitability, gripped Gemma as Gabriel walked alongside her, as sleek and muscular as a big cat, easily keeping pace.

From the moment she had realized that the kiss had been a mistake, she had done her best to distance herself from him. The last thing she needed right now was a resurgence of the old crush, the old love, that had haunted her for so long, but the plain fact was that right now she needed his help.

The wind gusted off the dark expanse of sea that glittered beneath a half-moon, raising gooseflesh on her arms and intensifying the sense of reliving a past that was emotionally fraught with temptation and risk.

Setting her jaw, she tried not to shiver and wished she had thought to bring a wrap. Unfortunately, when she had left her room at the Atraeus Resort, her home for the past few days, she hadn't been in any state to remember sensible details. She had been too stressed with the whole crazy idea that Zane was the answer to her problems.

Acutely aware of Gabriel next to her, his brooding glance touching on her profile, Gemma skimmed the parking lot and wondered which of the vehicles belonged to him.

She expected him to indicate one of the sedans that gleamed expensively under the lights, maybe a BMW or an Audi, but when he depressed a key and the lights of a muscular, low-slung Maserati flashed, the impression she had gained earlier was intensified. As ordered and high-powered as Gabriel's occupation was, there was nothing either soft or conventional about him. Underneath the business suit, he was utterly male, with the sleek, hard muscle and seasoned toughness that was uncompromisingly alpha.

Even though she had known how he could be, how he had been six years ago, the car put Gabriel firmly in context. She had gotten used to viewing him as belonging in the past, no longer connected with either her or Sanchia's life.

Now, suddenly, that convenient fantasy had evaporated. Gabriel was here, now, larger than life and twice as potent.

She drew in a breath at a sudden thought. And like it or not, according to the press story that would probably be published in the next few days, he was now part of her life.

Gabriel opened the passenger-side door and waited for her to climb into the dimly glowing interior. Forced to throw caution to the wind, at least until she was safely back in her hotel room, Gemma settled into an ultralow seat that smelled expensively of leather and felt like a warm, very expensive cloud.

Chilled from the breeze and inescapably on edge, she

quickly fastened her seat belt before Gabriel could offer to do it for her.

She shoved the light-colored bag, which seemed to glow in the dark, against her door, as far from Gabriel's view as she could get it. When she got back to her room, she intended to throw the entire thing away, bag, contents and all. It would take her a long time to forget the embarrassment and humiliation of the evening; the last thing she needed was reminders.

Gabriel slid into the driver's seat, making the interior of the Maserati seem even smaller. Seconds later, they were accelerating past the floodlit front of the Castello with its soaring stone facade and circular drive and down a narrow winding road.

Twin stone posts glided past as Gabriel turned onto the coast road and headed into the township of Medinos. Cupped in a gently curving bay, backed by arid, ridged hills, Medinos glittered softly. Lights from rows of streetlamps that resembled glowing pearls and ultramodern high-rises splashed out across the water, illuminating the graceful lines of yachts.

Gabriel braked for a set of lights. "I take it you're staying at the resort."

His deep, cool voice made her start. "For the meantime. I fly back to New Zealand in a couple of days."

Although she intended to change her ticket and leave on the earliest flight she could get. Tomorrow, if possible.

After the episode with Zane, and the next media scandal looming, she needed to get home to Sanchia as soon as she could.

Her fingers clenched together in her lap at the way all of her plans had flown to pieces. The thought that the child welfare people could try to take Sanchia permanently filled her with desperate fear. Until she got home, and had Sanchia back in her arms, she wouldn't be able to relax.

"I heard you've quit the job with the Atraeus Group."

"That's right." Warily, she juggled how much to tell him. "I need to be closer to my family. And I need a more settled environment for Sanch—for my child."

She felt rather than saw his gaze on her. "I take it your mother is caring for—the child?"

She didn't miss his slight hesitation, and, out of the blue, wrenching guilt jabbed at her. The moment was disorienting. Sanchia was his, and he didn't even know he had a daughter.

When she had been nursing her hurt and bearing the pregnancy on her own she had managed to convince herself that it was for the best, but now, in Gabriel's presence, the full weight of the deception settled in. The very least she could do was to give him her name. "Mom was looking after Sanchia, until she had a heart attack. One of my sisters has her at the moment."

"And that's why you've left your job."

Surprise at his knowledge made her stiffen. The wariness that she'd felt back at the Castello returned full force. "That's right. I was going to bring Sanchia out to Medinos, but now a lot of things have changed and I…need to go home."

Gabriel smoothly overtook a slower vehicle. "And your mother, is she okay?"

The concern in his voice reminded her that as much as she had tried to ignore Gabriel's existence, that didn't alter the fact that back in Dolphin Bay they were practically neighbors. "Mom's recovering. It wasn't a serious attack, more a warning. She just has to take things easy for a while."

"If there's anything I can do, let me know."

"Thank you for the offer. Luckily Mom has medical insurance, so she's had no problem with meeting costs."

The conversation reminded her that Gabriel had lost his father suddenly. The car accident had happened shortly after the night they had spent together. She could still remember anxiously scanning the newspapers for news of him and his family, and checking the internet to see what details she could pick up.

With relief Gemma saw the resort's neon sign. Gabriel pulled into the lobby parking lot just as a tall, familiar figure strode out of the front entrance.

Gemma's heart almost stopped in her chest. Zane.

He was too intent on his own agenda to notice them as he climbed into the Ferrari parked at the curb and shot away. Gemma skimmed the lighted hotel entrance looking for press. She couldn't see any, but she wasn't taking any chances. If Zane was here, the media were bound to be, also. The last thing she wanted to do now was walk into the lobby and get snapped.

She directed Gabriel around to the parking lot at the rear of the staff accommodation. As he slotted the Maserati into a space, Gemma's stomach tensed as the reporter who had followed her at the Castello stepped out of a rental car, camera in hand. He was accompanied by a second reporter, who was holding a video camera.

Gabriel frowned. "It's getting a little crowded around here. What do you want to do?"

She absolutely did not want to run into the media again, tonight. "Leave."

Zane and reporters was a combination she couldn't afford, which meant she couldn't stay at the Atraeus Resort tonight.

She could try requesting security, which she had needed

on occasion in her job as Zane's PA. But after what had happened at the Castello and the fact that she had officially resigned, she had to consider the possibility that Zane had advised his people that as she was no longer on the pay-roll, her status was as a guest only.

Before she could suggest another hotel, Gabriel reversed and cruised across the parking lot. The cameraman turned at the low throaty growl of the Maserati, but by the time he had lifted the camera and aimed it in their direction, Gabriel had turned out onto the main highway.

Seconds later they were in the middle of town, with its milling tourists, street cafés and tavernas. Idling now, to avoid the occasional jaywalking pedestrian, Gabriel cruised along the waterfront. "Do you have a place you could stay? Any friends on Medinos?"

Still unnerved by the sighting of both Zane and the press crew that seemed to be stalking her, Gemma kept her gaze on the ranks of gleaming cars parked along the street, the brightly dressed tourists mingling with the much more conventional Medinians. "No. When I've stayed in Medinos, I've always been working. I've spent most of my time either at the airport or the resort."

And any spare time she had spent either studying, talking with Sanchia via the internet or troubleshooting endless problems with nannies.

Gabriel took a turn into a quieter section of town, dotted with villas. "I have a beachside villa with a security gate. If you want to stay the night you're welcome."

Gemma risked a glance at Gabriel's profile. With his longer hair and the faint shadow of stubble on his jaw, he looked far more broodingly dangerous and exotically Medinian than she remembered.

The thought of spending further time with him in a private setting with no one but perhaps an odd servant around tightened the tension humming through her. Although with the Ambrosi Pearls launch it was entirely possible there would be other family members staying. "I was thinking a small *pensionato*."

Gabriel pulled over against the curb and stopped. "Unless you've prebooked one, you might have trouble getting a room. It's the height of the tourist season, plus there are a lot of press and extra people on the island for the Ambrosi Pearls launch."

He lifted a brow. "And unless you've got some extra clothing, even if you find a room, you could still have a problem with that scenario."

Gemma's stomach sank. She had temporarily forgotten that Medinos was a place that hadn't quite shaken off its medieval traditions, particularly with regard to women. Caught halfway between the east and west, no bikinis, and no cleavage or overtly sensual clothing were allowed in public areas. Unless in a private setting, which the Castello had been, women were expected to dress modestly.

Until she could either get into her room at the resort, or go shopping, all she had to wear was what she had on. No respectable *pensionato*—and that was the only kind on Medinos—would rent her a room while she was wearing a black lace dress and high heels, and with no luggage.

Although her bag, despite holding champagne and a negligee, could pass for luggage.

Gabriel extracted his phone from his pocket. "If you want I can ring a couple of places."

"Okay."

Fifteen minutes and ten calls later, Gabriel set the phone down. "The offer of a bed at my place is still good."

Gemma stared out of the Maserati's window and tried not to feel a forbidden jolt of excitement that she would be extending her time with Gabriel. "All I need is a bed for a few hours."

It was the lesser of two evils.

Just one night. How dangerous could that be?

Seven

A small thrill shot down Gemma's spine as Gabriel's villa, which occupied the bay next to Medinos's central business district, loomed in the darkness. Set against the pure dark backdrop of sea and sky, it was an arresting mixture of ancient and modern. The crenellated stone tower of an old fortress blended seamlessly with the blunt addition of smoothly rendered walls, the windows stark sheets of glass.

The view slid away as Gabriel drove into a cavernous, empty garage. As the remote-controlled door came down behind them, Gemma unbuckled her belt and climbed out of the car, eager to assert her independence before Gabriel could get around to open her door.

Grabbing her bag, she tried to suppress a renewed surge of awareness. Desperate to at least give the appearance of normality, she examined the garage space, which was big enough to hold at least four cars. It was empty, but that could be because everyone was out for the night. "Does your family stay here?"

Gabriel closed the door of the Maserati with a quiet thunk. "No. This is something in the nature of a retreat for me. My family usually arranges their own accommodations."

Her heart beat once, hard. So they really would be alone.

Despite her determination to be brisk and superficial, to clamp down on the spellbinding intensity of the attraction, she found herself once again caught in the net of Gabriel's gaze. Despite the fact that, in theory, Gabriel shouldn't have the least interest in her, the sense of being herded was suddenly suffocatingly strong. "I guess that explains why your mother was at the Atraeus Resort."

His gaze sharpened. "You saw my mother at the Atraeus Resort?"

"I helped settle her and her friend into their room."

He opened a door that led out onto a covered deck and gestured that she precede him. "Mom mentioned she had seen someone who looked like you, but she couldn't be sure because you've lost so much weight."

Gemma frowned, remembering the awkwardness of the scene. Although most of that had been generated by the shock she'd received when she'd heard that Gabriel was about to be engaged.

The remembrance of that made her stiffen. In all the turmoil of the night, the tingling heat of the kiss they'd shared, she had managed to gloss over the fact that Gabriel wasn't free. "I didn't think your mother recognized me."

Feeling suddenly depressed, she stopped at a heavy door and looked upward at old fortress rock, weathered by time. "This looks like an old watchtower."

"It's the remnants of the Messena Fortress, given to an

ancestor during the Crusades. It was a crumbled ruin even before the bombing in the Second World War."

Without waiting for him, she grasped the heavy iron ring and attempted to open a door that looked ancient and clunky.

When the door didn't budge, Gabriel stepped in. "Unless you know the security codes, you're going to have to let me do that."

Lifting a metal flap fitted into a niche in the rock wall, he pressed in the key and alarm codes. The lock disengaged with a smooth click.

As she pushed the door open into pooling silence, despite her confusion another electrifying thrill shot up Gemma's spine. At the Castello there had been people everywhere. Now there were no reporters, no pressure, just the two of them and the night.

A sense of inevitability heightened all of Gabriel's senses as Gemma stepped into the ancient watchtower, now a wine cellar filled with extremely expensive wines. He flicked a switch. Soft golden light filled the room, highlighting the rich color of Gemma's hair, the creaminess of her skin, and he was gripped by the conviction that in the space of a few minutes his life had swung in a totally new direction.

He had felt that kind of internal shift before, the night his father had died. That night had been marked by grief and grim resolve. The way he presently felt was the exact opposite. The calm deliberation that had become his hallmark had utterly deserted him and in its place was a humming, restless energy.

A cliché or not, he knew the exact moment the change had taken place: when he had seen Gemma across the width of the crowded reception room.

Stepping inside, he swung the heavy door, with its medieval double thickness of timbers designed to stop both arrows and spears, closed behind him. The sound of the lock reengaging echoed.

Gemma, who was already at the far end of the circular room that opened out at one end into a large barnlike lounge, was busy checking out the impressive view across the sea. She swung around, her expression professionally brisk. Gabriel couldn't help thinking that it was a look he had gotten used to seeing from his own very efficient PA.

"If it was anyone else, I might suspect your motives in locking the door."

"I'll take that as a compliment." Although Gabriel's sense of irritation increased that, evidently, even Gemma didn't think he was capable of doing anything either remotely edgy or borderline. Strolling to the wine counter, he poured some of the water, which was still sitting there from his afternoon session with Constantine, into two clean glasses. "What makes you so sure I don't have motives?"

Gemma gave him a preoccupied look, as if her attention had just switched to something else. "It's been six years since we last met. I seem to remember you saying that we had very little in common, so I don't see how that's changed."

"We did have one thing in common."

She checked her watch, although her cheeks had taken on a pink tinge, so she wasn't entirely oblivious to their exchange. "I don't think sex counts."

It did in his world. "So any motives on my part other than chivalry are doubtful?"

Her blush deepened. "It's been six years. You never called. I think that about settles it."

Gabriel frowned. Thinking about what Gemma might have needed from him was not an aspect he had dwelled on, because he'd been so absorbed with fixing the scandal that had erupted after his father's death. But he was thinking about it now. "Did you want me to call?"

Her gaze locked with his for an electrifying moment. "I slept with you. That was not something I did lightly. Of course I wanted you to call."

Blinking, as if she couldn't quite believe that she had said the words, Gemma set the bag, which she was still keeping annoyingly close, down beside one of two leather chairs grouped around a coffee table.

"I thought about calling." And a couple of times it had been more than that. He had actually picked up the phone and started pressing numbers before he had come to his senses.

She sent him a level look. "It wasn't a problem. I understood why you couldn't afford to be involved with me. Banks and scandal don't really go together."

Gemma began investigating the racks of wine lining the walls as if she were riveted by his wine collection. Gabriel suppressed a surge of frustration. It was not the response he'd hoped for.

She pulled out a bottle of a rare French vintage worth a staggering amount of money. "I know for a fact that if anything about you appears in the papers, it's always in the financial, not the social pages."

Suddenly intensely irritated at the way Gemma insisted on reinforcing his image as a staid, boring banker, Gabriel drained his water and set the glass down on the counter with a click. "I didn't know you were interested in the financial pages."

She gave the label of the award-winning burgundy a distracted look and slipped the bottle back onto the rack. "When I'm stuck on a long haul flight, I've been known to read anything I can get my hands on, even the financial pages."

She glanced at the narrow watch on her wrist again, and despite the optimism that had gripped him when Gemma had agreed to spend the night at his house, his mood plummeted. "One step up from the classified ads."

"Only just." She abandoned her perusal of the wine racks and strolled over to the counter. "Speaking of finances, I read somewhere that you're a qualified economist as well as an accountant—"

"With a calculator for a heart, no doubt."

She accepted the glass he handed her. "I didn't say that. If you had a calculator for a heart you wouldn't have bothered to rescue me. Twice."

His pulse racing that she had mentioned the previous occasion that he had intervened to help her, he said, "Just a suggestion, but maybe you need to rethink the kind of guy you're dating."

The second the words were out, he wished he could retract them. Six years on from the one passionate night they'd shared and he was sounding like an older brother—worse, a father figure—dispensing advice.

"I intend to. As of tonight, I'm not dating anyone afraid of commitment—"

The distinctive chime of her phone distracted Gemma from a conversation and a simmering tension that was continually pushing her out of her depth. She had been worried because Sanchia was due to call her and she absolutely could not take the call right now.

Feeling under siege, she dug the phone out of her evening purse, intending to simply turn it off. Sanchia would understand. She knew that Gemma couldn't always answer, and that she would pick up on the missed call when she could.

The phone ringing was a sharp reminder that she could not afford another sizzling fling with Gabriel. Before she could hit the power button, the phone was whisked out of her hand. Incensed, Gemma grabbed at the phone, desperate to get it back. "That's mine."

"You can have it back once Zane's hung up."

"Why would Zane be ringing me?"

Gabriel's gaze was cool and flat. "I'm not prepared to take any chances."

The small silence that followed, the knowledge that Gabriel was not only acting unreasonably, he was behaving in a distinctly possessive way, made her stomach clench.

Although she refused to accept that Gabriel's disconcerting focus on her was either real or lasting. She knew now that Zane and Lilah had found the kind of deep, committed love she herself longed for. She wished them well with all of her heart, but that didn't change the fact that their togetherness underlined her single, lonely—and now desperate—state. "I'm not Zane's girlfriend or his mistress."

Gabriel's expression underlined his disbelief. Given that he had dropped her like a hot coal six years ago, his opinion shouldn't register, but tonight it did.

She was tired of being judged and dismissed and treated as if she was a pretty airhead just out for a good time. She was strong and independent; she had dreams and desires and plans. She certainly wasn't the good-time girl the tabloids had dubbed her.

Just the thought of that derogatory label made her feel sick. The only good time she'd ever had had lasted just a few short hours. "I am not interested in an affair with Zane. If only you knew, it's the last thing I want."

One final chime and the call went through to answer phone.

She drew an impeded breath. She should be angry that Gabriel was behaving so high-handedly in taking her phone and switching it off. That he could believe, even now, after everything that had happened, that she would try to remain in contact with Zane.

But she couldn't sustain the anger for one simple reason. Gabriel wouldn't behave in such an arrogant fashion if he didn't care. The thought clutched at her deep inside and refused to let go, generating a dangerous excitement she recognized only too well. She lifted her chin. "And if Zane does call, what then?"

"I'll deal with him."

"It's none of your business, but the number that flashed up was my sister's, in Dolphin Bay. She's looking after Sanchia until I get home."

She caught the flash of relief in Gabriel's gaze and in that moment a startling thought hit her. Gabriel was jealous. The revelation took root, spiraled through her on a dizzying wave of delight.

So it definitely wasn't chance that he had used the secret tunnel that had come out near Zane's door. He must have deduced where she had gone and had probably chosen the hidden way to avoid the press.

He let out a breath, dragged long fingers through his hair, his expression repentant enough as he handed her the phone that she had to resist the urge to smile. "Damn. Sorry."

And just like that they were back to the softness, the singular, sweet camaraderie that in tiny fragments they'd shared over the years, and which she had always adored.

She drew in a breath at the curious melting sensation inside, the crazy desire to step close to Gabriel and test out her theory by winding her arms around his neck, lifting up on her toes and kissing him again.

Feeling suddenly in need of air, she turned to the French doors behind her, fumbled at the handle and stepped outside.

The fresh, cool night air took her breath as she walked to the edge of the balcony and looked out to sea and a magnificent view of the nearest island, Ambrus. Anything to dissipate the perilous warmth, the heady tension that gripped her.

Below the balcony a sweep of floodlit lawn flowed to a wild, rock-strewn garden, then down to a smooth stretch of sand. Further out dark clouds blotted out the stars. A gust of wind, a forerunner of the distant storm, sent strands of hair drifting around her cheeks and raised gooseflesh on her bare arms.

In the instant she felt cold, Gabriel's jacket dropped around her shoulders, the weight of it deliciously warm, a hint of his clean masculine scent clinging to the fine dark weave.

Grateful for the warmth, she resisted the urge to meet his gaze and succumb to that particular madness again. She'd gone to the Castello tonight needing a knight in shining armor. Instead, she was here on an ancient watchtower balcony with the fascinatingly dangerous Gabriel Messena, the last man she had thought she would ever be alone with again.

Worse, she was feeling every one of the tingling symptoms of attraction that she had tried to feel for Zane, and failed.

Desperate to break what was becoming an uncomfortable silence, Gemma checked her wristwatch and quickly texted Sanchia. She knew it was late on Medinos and that Gemma could possibly be asleep, so she wouldn't be too worried if Gemma didn't call back right away.

She tried for a bright, relaxed smile as she hugged his jacket around her, soaking in the warmth. "Thank you. I guess I'm still acclimating."

Gabriel crossed his arms over his chest and leaned against the parapet, looking sleek and muscular and as graceful as a big cat. With his dark hair blowing around clean-cut cheekbones, he looked utterly at ease in the stark Mediterranean landscape. "If you want to know why I helped you, it's because I saw a piece about you and Zane in a newspaper. I felt responsible, since I was the one who originally recommended you for the job."

Gemma frowned at Gabriel's alleged involvement in her landing the Atraeus job in Sydney four years ago. Originally, it had been for a PA position in one of the Sydney hotels. She had thought at the time that it had been a minor miracle that she had beaten off a number of better-qualified applicants but she would never in her wildest dreams have imagined that Gabriel had helped her out. "I thought it was Elena Lyon who put in a reference."

Elena was a girlhood friend, also from Dolphin Bay, and well known to the Messena family, since her aunt had been the housekeeper who was supposed to have had the affair with Gabriel's father. Although Elena swore black and blue that the affair was nothing more than supposition and media hype.

Gabriel lifted his shoulders. "Maybe she did, but Constantine approved the appointment on my recommendation."

Gemma firmly suppressed a surge of pleasure that Gabriel hadn't forgotten about her altogether, that he'd cared enough about her to ensure she obtained a good job. "In that case, thank you, but I still don't understand why you thought you had to intervene then or now. I'm well used to looking after myself."

Gabriel was silent for a beat. "I'm sure you are. But what about the father you need for your child?"

Eight

Gemma froze. Her first thought was that he knew Sanchia was his, but then the way he had referred to her registered.

He had said "your child," not his child. Which meant he had probably read one of the gossipy snippets of information the tabloids had recently printed. Snippets which had implied that Zane was the father and thankfully hadn't included any real details about Sanchia, such as her age. The reporters had been more interested in repeating known facts about Zane rather than far less interesting facts about either herself or her daughter.

For a few taut seconds, the urge to confess to Gabriel that Sanchia was his was strong enough that she actually opened her mouth to speak, but the caution that had gripped her ever since the last nanny had accused her of being an unfit mother reasserted itself.

The custody situation was difficult enough without introducing the complication of Sanchia's biological father.

"That's why you intervened? Because you thought Zane wouldn't be interested in fatherhood?"

Gabriel frowned. "I intervened because I was the one who put you in a situation where you came into Zane's sphere of influence in the first place."

Gemma gripped the lapels of Gabriel's jacket, hugging it more closely against the wind, although that was a mistake, because the movement released more of his clean, masculine scent.

She went back to the issue of just how she had gotten her job. "What makes you so sure I wouldn't have gotten the job purely on merit?"

"Constantine wanted someone who could be trusted with confidentiality. I told him you could."

If Gemma had felt chilled before, she was warming up fast. Gabriel probably thought he was pouring oil on troubled waters, but as far as she was concerned it was more like pouring gasoline on a smoldering fire. "You mean I got the job because I kept quiet about sleeping with you?"

Her throat had automatically locked against the phrase *one-night stand*. Maybe it hadn't been special for him, but she had been caught up in the fairy-tale magic of the night, the indefinable feeling that the gorgeous man who had come to her rescue was special.

He shrugged. "A lot of people are affected by wealth. They have an agenda. That didn't seem to be the case with you."

She frowned at his summation of her character, even though it was on the positive side. Maybe it was simply that his view of her was so objective. She couldn't help thinking that if he had ever been even the tiniest bit in love with her, he wouldn't have seen her in such a cold, impersonal light.

Like an employee.

It highlighted an aspect of Gabriel's character that she had suspected had always been there. That in his heart of hearts, Gabriel valued control and slotting people into neat boxes more than he valued spontaneous love and affection.

It explained why his mother had thought he would accept a marriage to a well-connected, suitably rich and beautiful girl.

Suddenly, the idea that Gabriel could judge her for possibly wanting to make a good marriage, when it was obviously standard practice within the Messena family, made her bristle. "So you thought I had an agenda, as in trying to marry the boss."

His gaze narrowed warily. "It happens."

"And sometimes the agenda works the other way. There are plenty of employees who get sexually harassed."

"Point taken."

The piercing look Gabriel gave her made her feel distinctly uncomfortable and she hastily decided that it was time to drop this subject. He was referring to the relationship he thought she'd had with Zane, but the last thing she wanted him to do was remember back to what had happened six years ago and figure out that *he* could be the father. "Why should you care, anyway?"

He crossed his arms over his chest, and she had the distinct sense that she had been neatly maneuvered. "Because I have a proposition for you. You need a fiancé to get Sanchia back, and as it happens, I need one to short-circuit a clause in my father's will."

In clipped phrases he explained the glitch with the will that his uncle was presently exploiting in order to pressure Gabriel into a marriage he didn't want.

An absurd sense of relief gripped her at the explanation that Gabriel wasn't in love with some beautiful, perfect woman, but was trying to avoid an arranged marriage. It also cast a new light on his pursuit of her tonight that made a depressing kind of sense. He wasn't after her because of passion, but business.

Gabriel shrugged. "To cut a long story short, if you'll agree to be my fiancée for the period of time it takes me to gain full control of the bank, in exchange I can offer you an apartment, a job and whatever else you need to get your daughter back."

The offer was riveting, but tempted as she was to grab it, she couldn't ignore the danger of getting too close to Gabriel. "How long would you need me to pose as your fiancée?"

"A week at most. That should be enough time to convince the legal firm that handles the trust provision of the will."

Her mind was racing. She could do it. She could be Gabriel's fake fiancée for a week. After all, she was trained to act. How hard could it be? She drew a swift breath. "What kind of job?"

"The same thing you did for the Atraeus Group. The reason I came to Medinos was to meet with Constantine. He's starting up a new branch of Ambrosi Pearls in Auckland. I'll be taking care of the launch phase. We start advertising for staff next week."

Still feeling skittish and cautious, despite Gabriel offering her everything on her current wish list, Gemma took a deep breath and let the idea settle in. It was a new venture with an old established firm like Ambrosi, and the kind of opening she would have wanted to apply for anyway. The fact that Gabriel was only involved in the start-up phase meant that she could keep the job after their charade ended, which would be perfect.

With a new job and an apartment. It would mean that she could get Sanchia back immediately.

Before she could change her mind, Gemma said, 'Yes."

The momentary flash of surprise in Gabriel's gaze startled her. "You thought I was going to refuse."

"It crossed my mind, since the job combines a personal relationship with employment."

"I do believe there's a line drawn in the sand. It's called a personal contract."

A hint of impatience jerked his brows together. "Yes, but in this case we have a verbal agreement that the initial stages of this job involve some personal connection."

The startled recognition that Gabriel wanted more than just a charade set off alarm bells, although the alarm was almost totally drowned by a tingling heat that was dangerous.

She cleared her throat and tried to keep her tone smooth and professional. After all, Gabriel had just employed her as his PA. "Of course. Definitely. Within certain bounds."

And the first rule would be that if they were going to proceed, she needed to protect herself emotionally.

"Good." Gabriel's hands closed around her arms as he drew her slowly, mesmerisingly closer. "We have an understanding."

Gemma stiffened at the warmth of his touch, the instant fiery desire that swamped her. Somewhere in the back of her mind languished the concept that sleeping with the boss before they even got to the office was a very bad idea. "I'm not exactly sure what I understand."

"I guess what I'm trying to say is that I've always regretted what happened six years ago."

The words she had wanted to hear all those years ago shimmered through her, undermining every one of her reservations. "You can't be serious?"

Reaching out, he linked his fingers with hers and pulled her closer and, like a fool, unable to resist him, she went.

The warmth of his breath drifted against her throat. "Why not?"

Because it was too late for the luxury of the wild, fatal attraction that was zinging through her. Too late for a re-play of what had happened six years ago: the starry night, the champagne. The rescue.

She drew a swift breath. And all of those things followed by the off-the-register lovemaking.

The kind of lovemaking she would in all likelihood never again experience, because realistically, the type of man she would end up marrying would be a dependable, average kind of guy who placed a high value on family. He wouldn't be either dangerously attractive or mega-wealthy. First off, Sanchia would have to like him.

A deep feeling of depression hit her at the thought that marriage with someone else would ultimately be dependent on Sanchia's needs, not hers. That it would be an up-hill struggle to find someone other than Gabriel who she could settle for.

Until that moment she hadn't understood just how vivid and exceptional her response to Gabriel was.

Resolutely, she reminded herself of the non-negotiable list of things she needed to establish in her life over the next few weeks. She could not allow herself to be sucked back into a dream that had already proved to have no substance.

Lifting her chin, she met the cool determination of Gabriel's gaze. "I didn't think that what happened had meant that much to you. After all, it was only one night."

"A night I've never forgotten."

The deep timbre of his voice shivered through her. One more half step and he was so close she could feel the heat flowing off his big body, catch the scent of his skin. He cupped her chin, hesitated, then lowered his mouth to hers.

The kiss, his lips soft, was little more than a touch, a tester, but suddenly her heart was pounding and she was having difficulty breathing.

She considered what he was offering, right here, right now. Another passionate interlude.

But the sting of that thought was drowned out by another much more powerful consideration. Despite wanting to move on from the powerful attraction that drew her to Gabriel, she hadn't; she still wanted him.

Everything was in place, the starry night sky, the sea, the sense of isolation and privacy, and somewhere inside a too-comfortable couch or very large bed. It was a virtual replay of the night six years ago.

A gust of wind tugged at his hair, and the moon slid behind a cloud. As the gloom of the approaching squall deepened, he cupped her face.

The pads of his thumbs swept over her cheeks, sending rivulets of fire shimmering through her. "Say yes."

She froze in the rawness of the moment, the flash of need that melted her bones.

Her hair whipped around her cheeks. The night was turning wild and elemental. If she wanted to keep things on a professional basis, she should go, hand his jacket back and walk up to the road before the approaching deluge hit. She had her phone; she could order a taxi or ring the hotel concierge, who would send someone to pick her up. But she knew that she wouldn't be doing any such thing, and suddenly there was no air. "Yes."

In answer, Gabriel dipped his head and laid his mouth on hers. Emboldened, she dropped her phone in Gabriel's jacket pocket and braced her hands on his shoulders. The warmth from the muscle beneath her palms sent a quiver of heat through her, as flash after flash of memories from that long-ago night turned the air molten. Heart pounding, she lifted up on her toes, wrapped her arms around his neck and kissed him back.

Her faint awkwardness, the fear that he would know just how unpracticed she was at this, disappeared as his arms tightened around her waist. The heat from his body burned through the thin lace and silk of her dress as she shifted closer still.

The fierce desire she couldn't afford cascaded through her along with a sudden clear memory of exactly what had seduced her six years ago. Apart from the dark and dangerous outer package, Gabriel had been unexpectedly gentle.

He had gone to some lengths to make sure that nothing happened that she didn't want. They had slow danced, they had laughed and then they had walked along the beach and ended up on the tiny adjacent island, which was reached by a causeway.

The only slip-up had been when they had both lost control and had ended up making love without protection. Even then, Gabriel had apologized. And when they had spent the rest of the night snuggled together just talking she had felt dizzyingly, almost terrifyingly, happy.

In some indefinable way they had connected. For want of a better word, Gabriel had been nice, which was why it had hurt so much when he hadn't ever followed up.

Out at sea lightning flashed and the damp pressure of the wind increased. Not in the least intimidated, instead drawn by the primitive fierceness of the storm, the clean, simple, uncomplicated nature of it, she fitted herself even closer to Gabriel.

Rain spattered, shockingly cold against her overheated skin. Gabriel lifted his head and muttered something short in liquid Medinian.

A split second later the heavens opened up, the deluge soaking. The world tilted as Gemma found herself lifted and cradled in Gabriel's arms. Two long strides and they were inside. The sharp thud of the door slamming behind them punctuated the wild turn the night had taken.

Gemma's feet found the floor and Gabriel's jacket slipped off her shoulders. She registered the faint clunk of her phone, which was in the jacket pocket. She dragged chilled fingers through her hair, which clung to her skin like damp seaweed.

Gabriel stayed her hand. "Let me do that."

In contrast to the fury outside, his touch, as he smoothed her hair back into some semblance of order, was gentle and deliberate. But it wasn't what she wanted.

It had been six years since they had made love, years in which she'd been busy and fulfilled with work, study and parenting, but where, essentially, she'd remained alone.

She had tried to resurrect her dating life, but somehow she just hadn't had the enthusiasm for any of the very nice men she had occasionally dated. As hard as she'd tried she hadn't wanted anyone, until now. One glance from Gabriel and every nerve ending in her body had been humming.

With fingers that felt clumsy and inept, she dragged at the buttons of his shirt until it hung open over a broad chest and mouthwateringly tight abs. He shrugged free of the damp shirt, tossing it on the floor, then pulled her close and kissed her.

His hands framing her hips, he walked her backward. The quality of the light changed as they traversed the lamp-lit sitting room and entered a darker, quieter room.

An enormous bed, piled with pillows and draped in an ornate, burnished coverlet, floated on a sea of dark oak floorboards, dominating a bedroom that was an arresting mixture of modern severity and lavish excess.

She felt the loosening of her dress as the zip released. Anxiety gripped her at the thought of being naked with

Gabriel after all this time, of the mechanics of making love after years of being emotionally and sexually closed down. She might have been stuck in a time warp, but he hadn't, and her inadequacies were abruptly choking.

She sensed his frown rather than saw it. "What's wrong?"

"It's been a while."

"How long?"

She ducked her head against his shoulder, her face burning. "Since—the pregnancy."

He pulled her close, fitting her against the muscled contours of his body and the awkwardness shimmered into heat. Soothed by the dimness, she eased her arms out of the shoulder straps and let her dress drop to the floor.

His fingers threaded into her damp hair, tilted her face back so he could look into her eyes. To her surprise, his mouth was quirked in a half smile. "Don't worry. You might have forgotten, but I haven't."

Nine

When he murmured that there was no rush, that they could take their time, she reached for a trace of the old levity, the fun side of her that had shriveled when the custody situation with Sanchia had blown up. "Are you telling me you're slow?" Her own experience was that he was fast, hot and selective.

"Not where you're concerned." He grinned as he dipped his head and nibbled on her lobe, and her brain temporarily froze.

Emboldened by the humor and the sweetness, she leaned into him, wrapped her arms around his waist and soaked in his heat, his delicious scent.

She felt her bra strap release. In a definitely slick move he dispensed with the bra, leaving her in just her panties, and cupped her breasts. Her breath hitched in her throat. "That was sneaky."

He grinned, making her heart flip. "You should know by now that all guys are sneaky."

Bending his head he took her breast into her mouth. Sensation hummed through her, coiled low in her belly, and any awkwardness sizzled out of existence.

Gabriel lifted his head, fierce satisfaction registering. A split second later he picked her up and placed her on the bed then peeled out of his trousers before joining her.

Gabriel fully clothed was impressive; naked, he was beautiful. And, for the moment, *hers*. He let her touch him and shape him and learn the intriguing planes and angles of his body, the hard muscle and hair-roughened skin.

Keeping her close against the furnace heat of his body, he reached into the drawer of a bedside cabinet and found a condom. Lightning jagged through the sky, illuminating the room as he sheathed himself. Seconds later, when she stretched herself on him, the tension that had been slowly building wound unbearably tight.

His gaze locked with hers as he gripped her hips and she logged the fact that, as controlled as he was, Gabriel had been keeping his desire rigidly in check.

With easy strength he rolled so that he was on top. Tension coiled as she felt him lodge between her legs, the heavy pressure, the weight of him anchoring her to the bed.

Rain spattered on the wall of glass, filling the night with the rhythm of the storm. Heat and dampness seemed to explode, and suddenly the deep, achy throb low in her belly, the humid heat of the night was too much. Coiling her arms around Gabriel's neck, she pulled him closer, pressing up against him. With a hoarse groan and one heavy thrust he was inside her, the night dissolving, one with the wild storm, as they clung together.

* * *

Long minutes ticked by while they lay entwined. The storm passed, leaving behind a dripping quiet and the heavy roar of surf hitting the white sand beach below the house.

Gabriel pulled her close. This time he took charge, making love to her with a slow intensity that took her breath.

Long minutes later, sleep tugged at Gemma along with the knowledge that now that they had made love, it was going to be impossible to keep Gabriel at arm's length for the duration of their fake engagement.

Heat shimmered through her at the thought that they could make love again, that Gabriel wanted her. Making love had been a mistake: she'd known it, but it was too late now. The damage was done.

Her priority now had to be to concentrate on the professional aspects of the new job, which meant no sex. She needed to establish a working relationship with Gabriel that would fulfill the part he wanted her to play but that would not compromise her new job or her emotions.

Creating a professional distance was going to be tricky, especially with her willpower at such a low ebb, but it wasn't as if she hadn't coped without sex before.

She could do it, but after tonight she was aware it would take all of her acting skills.

Her last conscious thought was that the first thing she needed to do was leave. If she woke up with Gabriel they would make love again, which would be counterproductive. For now she would sleep, just for an hour....

Gabriel waited until Gemma's breathing evened out before gently disengaging himself from the arm draped across his midriff and climbing out of the rumpled bed.

The room was filled with a pressing darkness, barely

penetrated by the glow of a single lamp out in the lounge, but even so, he could clearly make out Gemma's form. Against the burnished coverlet, her pale skin glowed like a pearl and the rich flood of red hair, leached of its color, looked like ebony on his pillows.

He studied the pure line of Gemma's profile and the fierce need that had overtaken him earlier reasserted itself.

He wanted her, and he now knew how much she wanted him. The minute he'd kissed her earlier in the evening, the intervening years had seemed to dissolve, the chemistry instant and explosive.

Snagging his pants from the floor, he padded through to the bathroom, freshened up and pulled on the trousers. After draining a glass of water in the kitchen, he found Gemma's canvas bag where she'd left it in the wine cellar and carried it through to his study.

Closing the door behind him, he flicked on a lamp and set the bag on his desk. Setting the bottle of champagne down on the glossy surface, he drew out the liquid soft mass of black silk and lace. His stomach tightened as his guess that it was lingerie, not a wrap, was confirmed.

As he pulled out what was without doubt a pretty negligee, he noticed something fluttering and white. A sales tag that Gemma in her impulsive haste to seduce Zane had clearly forgotten to remove.

His fingers tightened on the garment, elation gripping him.

The negligee wasn't the symbol of a seasoned sexual relationship. It was new and unused.

It was the final confirmation.

The craziness of the night now made perfect sense. He understood Gemma's position, her need to draw Zane into a committed relationship.

She had failed. Zane had already been committed to

another woman, for which Gabriel was profoundly thankful. Because, as of an hour ago, as far as Gabriel was concerned, Gemma now belonged to him.

He noticed a glossy magazine in the bottom of the bag. Frowning, he pulled it out. It was folded open at an article, "How To Seduce Your Man in Ten Easy Moves." He flicked through it, skimming a collection of articles on what men really wanted and a list of exotic tactical dating maneuvers that were "guaranteed to succeed."

The evidence of the off-the-wall solutions Gemma had come up with to solve her custody problem should have been a turnoff. Instead it only proved just how unprepared and unpracticed Gemma was at making love. The magazine further underlined her lack of experience with men in general. He knew from what she'd told him that she hadn't made love since she'd gotten pregnant.

The thought of Gemma with a baby made his stomach tighten. Heated tension hummed through him. If the explosive attraction between them was not simply an obsessive sexual attraction and blossomed into an actual relationship, Gemma could one day be pregnant with his child.

The thought was out in left field, and that was where it would stay, he decided, until he was certain. He would not repeat his father's mistake by risking the calm order he had worked so hard to restore to the business and his family by succumbing to a searing attraction.

Gemma surfaced from a restless dream instantly aware of the warmth and weight of Gabriel's arm where it lay draped across her waist. A small sensual shock brought her fully awake as she registered the delicious heat of his body, the sheer intimacy of waking up and finding him sprawled next to her.

Glancing at the digital clock on the bedside table she

discovered that, despite trying to stay awake until Gabriel fell asleep, at some point she must have slept deeply, because it was now after five in the morning.

It was past time to go, although she was finding it unexpectedly difficult to revert to the businesslike mode she had decided was the only sensible way forward with this relationship.

Knowing she shouldn't, she turned her head on the pillow and studied Gabriel's face in the dimness of the early morning light. Hair tousled, his lashes inky crescents against olive skin, he looked younger, and uncannily like the Gabriel of six years ago.

Her heart squeezed tight in her chest. In sleep, he looked oddly vulnerable and she had to fight the urge to simply cuddle up to him and immerse herself in the simple pleasure of his heat and warmth. She had to keep reminding herself that Gabriel was no tame pussycat; if she gave an inch, he would take a mile. If she was going to manage her way safely through the next few days, without falling in love with him all over again, she would have to be strict with herself.

And the first rule, now that Gabriel was her boss and her soon-to-be fake fiancé, was no more sex. She had given in to him tonight because she simply hadn't been able to resist. She had felt starved of affection, starved of love. Maybe because of all the stress and the shock of the custody battle she had been unexpectedly vulnerable.

Whatever the cause, if she wanted to enforce the no-sex rule, she would have to leave now, before she was enticed back into his arms and lost her willpower altogether.

She intended to leave him a note, outlining her conditions. She was certain, given the businesslike way Gabriel had couched her new job description, that once he adjusted to the fact that she would not continue to sleep with him, that he would be happy with the idea.

Shifting slightly, just enough to dislodge Gabriel's arm, Gemma inched nearer the edge of the bed. Fully awake now, the chill of early morning registered. The gray light of dawn pushed through the enormous expanse of glass that framed the panoramic view of the Mediterranean, revealing the hedonistic chaos of the bedroom. Her clothes and Gabriel's were scattered where they had discarded them, and at some point the silk coverlet had slipped off the bed and now lay tumbled on the floor.

Outside the piercing cry of a gull was loud enough that Gemma held her breath as Gabriel stirred restlessly. The rumpled silk sheet slipped low on his hips, exposing his long muscular torso and the intriguing line of hair that arrowed to his loins.

Setting her jaw against the instant tug on her senses, and annoyed with herself that after years of abstinence she was actually fickle enough to let herself be ruled by desire, Gemma worked her way free of the gorgeous, entangling sheets. Her feet landed softly on the bare expanse of the hardwood floor, the cool of the marble-smooth wood sending an involuntary shiver through her.

Overpoweringly aware of her nakedness and the faint stiffness that telegraphed just what she had been doing for half the night, Gemma was tempted to drag the silk coverlet off the floor and pull it around herself as a covering. Reluctantly, she abandoned the idea. It was a miracle she hadn't woken Gabriel up already, and modesty came a bad second next to her need to leave and reestablish her collapsed boundaries.

Padding silently, she found her panties. As she straightened, she caught a ghostly view of herself in a carved gold full-length mirror. Her mind instantly slid back to the riveting, addictive pleasure she'd experienced making love with Gabriel. Cheeks warming, she scooped up her bra, which was dangling over the arm of a chair, and a little desperately reminded herself of the downside of all this.

Six years, and she had made the same mistake with the same guy, and once again without settling any of the vital issues, such as love and commitment. The only saving grace was that this time they had used contraception so she was safe from a second pregnancy.

Despite the fact that she absolutely did not want to get pregnant, the thought was oddly depressing, because it brought home the fact that as irresistible as the passion they had shared was, love had definitely not been involved.

It impressed upon her the need to stick to her resolve that there would be no more sex, because giving in would only signal to Gabriel that she would happily accept sex over love and commitment, that she didn't require him to value her.

When the fake engagement was over, she could work on forgetting Gabriel. She had done it before; she could do it again.

As she bent to pick up her lace dress, which lay pooled on the floor, her fingers brushed Gabriel's discarded shirt, which was lying next to it. Irresistibly tempted, she picked up the shirt instead.

The faint, clean masculine scent that clung to the fabric made her stomach clench on a zing of desire. Out of nowhere a shimmering wave of emotion hit her. If she'd had any sense she wouldn't have done such a silly, sentimental thing as picking up his shirt, but now that she had, she didn't want to relinquish it.

It was silly. She didn't need a memento of their time together. She would see Gabriel again in just a few days when she started at Ambrosi Pearls, but by then their relationship would be back on a proper professional footing. Apart from the necessities of the charade, there would be no more intimacy, no more passionate kisses, no more snuggling in bed. And absolutely no more sex.

Although, it was a fact that the shirt would be a more practical piece of clothing to wear on Medinos in broad daylight than the sexy lace gown.

A rustling sound, Gabriel turning over in bed, made her freeze in place. She risked a quick look. He was now lying sprawled on his stomach on the side of the bed she had vacated. In the gray light slanting across the bed, the long line of his back looked muscular and sleek, his tanned skin exotically dark against the white silk. From the even tenor of his breathing, and his utter, boneless relaxation, he had simply turned over and was unaware that she had left the bed.

Letting out a silent breath of relief, Gemma padded quickly from the room. Minutes later, she had found her bag and retrieved her phone from Gabriel's jacket pocket. She located a bathroom off the main living area. After using the facilities and washing her hands and face, she quickly dressed.

As she fastened the buttons of Gabriel's shirt, she checked the effect in the large vanity mirror. Gauzy and white, the shoulder seams fell halfway to her elbows and the shirttails covered her to her knees.

She tried not to notice the wild tousle of her hair, or the fact that her mouth was faintly swollen and there was a faint red patch on her neck where Gabriel's stubbled jaw must have scraped her skin.

A tinge of misery edged through her resolve as she rolled up the trailing shirt cuffs until they were bunched just above her wrists. The result wasn't stylish, but it was acceptable. She could easily be someone who had gone for an early morning swim and had decided to use a shirt as a cover-up.

Her heart leaped in her chest as she checked her wristwatch and saw how much time had passed. She still needed to write her note. If she was going to get out of the house before Gabriel woke up, she would have to hurry.

Not bothering to finger comb her hair, she picked up her bag and padded to the kitchen. Finding a piece of notepaper, she quickly dashed off an explanatory note. She included her email and phone numbers, anchored it on the counter with a cup then padded to the front door. Remembering to turn the alarm off, she eased the door open and stepped outside. Her heart hammered as she gently closed the door. Simultaneously, her phone chimed.

Sending a brief prayer upward that she had gotten out of the house before Sanchia rang, she answered the call as she walked quickly, avoiding the drive and instead heading for the beach. The route to town was more direct and it would be easier on her bare feet.

The conversation was grounding. It was a relief to put her own needs aside and think of Sanchia's instead, and for her daughter the equation was simple—she needed the security of her mother back in her life.

Gemma checked her watch again as she said good-night and ended the call. She then rang the airline and changed her flight. The extra cost made her stomach hollow out, but now that she had a job, she would be able to replenish her bank account.

A fifteen-minute walk to the hotel, and hopefully any press would still be in bed after the late night. She had an hour and a half until her flight. She had already done most of her packing, so all she really needed to do was pile the few things she'd left out into her case, zip it closed then catch a taxi. She would check in and board straight away.

Once she got to Sydney, she would sort all of the furniture and possessions she had left in storage, dispose of the things she didn't need and have the rest freighted to New Zealand.

Number two on her list of things to do was change her appearance. The idea was extreme, but she was tired of the media sneaking around after her, and with her stylish clothes and red hair she was just too easy to spot.

As long as her welfare caseworker knew she was engaged, there was no need for a media circus. She was determined that the move back home would be a complete fresh start, in all ways.

Tears welled as she walked along the pristine beauty of the shore, waves curling into foam at her feet. Dashing the moisture away, she kept her gaze on the distinctive shape of the Atraeus Resort, midway along the misted curve of the beach, and resisted the urge to look back.

She'd had a wonderful night and had said her own private emotional goodbyes to the relationship, such as it was. The small kernel of hurt that not once had Gabriel mentioned any degree of emotional involvement was the most difficult thing to acknowledge. Maybe he felt he hadn't needed to because it wasn't as if it was the first time they had made love, but the lack mattered to Gemma.

It underlined the need to enforce her own rules on the situation, and one of those was that if they were going to be engaged for a week, then during that time Gabriel would have to play his part. He would have to value her as if he *did* love her.

It was a small point, but it was important to Gemma. A man valuing his fiancée meant a ring, flowers, dinner— all of the important elements of a courtship that he had happily bypassed both times because she had slept with him so quickly.

* * *

Gabriel woke with the sun on his face and the space beside him in bed empty.

The second his lids flipped open he knew that Gemma wasn't just missing from his bed; she was gone.

He should have seen it coming, read it in the quiet way she had tried to distance herself from him in bed after making love. A distance he had obliterated by the simple expedient of wrapping an arm around her waist and drawing her close.

The first thing he saw as he climbed out of bed was her dress and shoes still on the floor. Padding through to the sitting room he noted that the canvas bag was gone, and the shirt he had tossed over the arm of a chair was missing.

He muttered something short and flat under his breath. After pulling on a pair of dark pants, he walked out onto the balcony. His jaw tightened as he noted the trail of footprints in the sand. Sliding his phone out of his pants pocket, he dialed the hotel and asked to be put through to security.

A brief conversation later, he hung up. He had thought Gemma might disappear for the day, but it was worse than that. She had just left for the airport.

Moving quickly, Gabriel walked through to the kitchen and found a note anchored to the counter. The message was simple, politely thanking him for the night together and stating the new terms of their relationship, which from now on, owing to Gemma's status as his employee, would not include sex.

Gabriel's fingers closed on the piece of paper, crumpling it. She had ditched him, close enough, and he hadn't seen it coming.

Although, thinking back, it was not the first time. Technically, he had ended their last relationship, but Gemma had never at any point tried to cling to him or get him back.

Six years ago she had seemed unruffled by the fact that he had no space for a relationship.

He smoothed out the crumpled note and reread it, frowning at the businesslike language, the small P.S. that stated that they would both have to play their roles as an engaged couple to the letter.

He frowned. What did that mean?

He was not exactly au fait with the whole process of getting engaged. As far as he was concerned this was just a sham that would facilitate his control of his company.

And keep Gemma in his bed until he could figure out just where the relationship was heading.

He finished dressing, not bothering with a shower and shave. By the time he accelerated away from the house, only fifteen minutes had passed since he had first woken up. Even so, he was certain he was going to be too late to catch Gemma.

As he drove, he dialed the airport. Precious minutes ticked away while the call was shuffled to someone more senior and manifests were checked. He had thrown his weight around and used every bit of influence he had, but by the time it was ascertained which of the international flights Gemma was on, the plane had been cleared for takeoff.

Pulling over onto the side of the winding coast road with its stunning views, Gabriel climbed out of the Maserati. Gaze narrowed against the glare of the sun, he searched the blue arc of the sky and saw the jet in the air.

The sea breeze whipped his hair around his jaw and flattened his shirt against his torso as he watched the jet for long seconds.

Despite all of the unanswered questions he had about Gemma, his unwillingness to commit, it was an out he didn't want.

Too late to realize he should have cossetted Gemma more, treated her like a date instead of rushing her into bed. His approach had lacked finesse; it had lacked even basic good manners.

But the problem was, he wasn't certain how much more he wanted from this relationship. All he knew was that Gemma had fascinated him six years ago, and she fascinated him now. They hardly knew each other, and both times the passion had been too quick, the situations pressurized. What they needed was the one thing they had never had: time together.

Although he had ensured that they would have that now.

Relief filled him that he had tied her to an employment contract. He had time on his side. After last night he was certain that, despite the odds, Gemma was emotionally involved. No woman could respond as she had and not be.

The addition to the note about playing their roles as an engaged couple slid back into his mind and a small, salient fact registered.

When he had flipped through the magazine in Gemma's holdall during the night, he had noticed a large section on women being valued in relationships, with passages underlined in blue ink as if Gemma had read and reread the article, committing it to memory.

He had made love to Gemma, and now she wanted to be courted.

Sliding behind the wheel of the Maserati, Gabriel put the car in gear and drove back toward Medinos.

Now that he had some facts to work with, he could form a strategy. He was a little rusty with dating, and it was a fact that he had never courted a woman, but he had a major advantage. Gemma had slept with him twice, despite his utter lack of courtship, which meant that she had a definite weakness he could, and would, exploit.

Sexually, she couldn't resist him.

Ten

Five days later, Gemma walked toward the plush ground-floor offices in Newmarket, Auckland, for her first day of work at the newest Ambrosi Pearl House.

Gleaming glass doors slid open, flashing back the conservative new image—she hesitated to call it an actual disguise—that she was still adjusting to.

Alarmed by the attention of the press when she had arrived in Sydney, and their interest in the fact that she was now, apparently, having a hot affair with Gabriel, she had made a beeline for her hairdresser and changed the color of her hair to a low-key sable brown.

Once she had made the initial breakthrough of changing her hair color, she had distilled the reinvention process down to rummaging through good quality secondhand shops for shoes and clothing in neutral shades. It had been a productive exercise because she had found a number of exquisitely cut, designer-label items for very cheap prices.

Evidently, this season no one wanted to be seen dead in either oatmeal or beige.

Today, instead of her normal clear, bright colors and fun lace and ruffles, she was wearing a biscotti suit. She refused to call the color beige. Fake glasses and her hair smoothed into a prim French pleat added to the office look.

But as boring as the color of the suit was, it wasn't as low-key as she would have liked. The jacket cinched in at the waist, emphasizing the fullness of her breasts and the curve of her hips. The skirt was also a little on the short side, making her legs look even longer. She had added high heels to the outfit, because she had made a judgment call and balanced the need to start her new job incognito against looking frumpy.

So far her new image had worked like a dream. No one had hounded her at the airport or tried to photograph her, and it was no wonder. When she had checked her appearance in the mirror that morning, she had barely recognized herself.

A workman wearing a faded gray tank, tanned, muscled biceps on show as he painted a wall, grinned at her and clutched at his heart as she strolled past.

Gemma found herself grinning back as she headed for the elevators and the second floor, where the offices were based. She just bet the guy was married with children—they all were—but the harmless bit of fun was soothing and exactly the lift she needed.

Boring in designer neutrals, but not dead in the water... yet.

Aware that she had almost veered into forbidden territory in thinking sexually about Gabriel, she refocused in a more positive direction.

Just that morning she had bought Sanchia a tiny hot-pink tutu and a pair of ballet slippers. She was going to give them to her once she had gotten the all-clear from the welfare caseworker and was able to move Sanchia back in with her. Now that she had a guaranteed income, she could afford the ballet lessons Sanchia wanted.

She pressed the call button on the elevator then stepped inside as the doors swished open. The sound of a firm tread behind her signaled that someone else had just entered the building.

She heard the low timbre of a masculine voice as the doors closed and froze, certain it was Gabriel.

On edge, she exited on the second floor and walked to the front desk. The receptionist, an elegant blonde called Bonny, was expecting her. Gemma glanced around as she followed Bonny through a smoothly carpeted corridor, amazed at the speed with which the new Ambrosi Pearls venture had been put together.

By the time she had reached Sydney, the employment contract had already been in her email in-box. All she'd had to do was print it out, sign it and fax it to the number supplied. Within an hour of doing so, she had received a flight ticket, which had surprised her, as there had been no mention that her travel expenses would be paid. The following day, she had received the lease to her new apartment in the mail, and had sent a certified copy off to her welfare caseworker.

Bonny introduced her to another very efficient older woman called Maris, who took her through to Gabriel's large, sleek office, which was dominated by a large mahogany desk. Although the most notable feature by far was that one wall contained a collection of computer screens flashing up nonstop financial information.

Maris indicated she should take a seat while she fetched

coffee, but Gemma, her gaze glued to the screens, was too wired to sit.

Moments later, Gabriel, larger than life and broodingly attractive in a dark suit, a pristine white shirt and a red tie knotted at his throat stepped into the office and closed the door behind him.

Despite coaching herself for this moment, her heart slammed in her chest and a highly inappropriate image of Gabriel naked and sprawled in silk sheets popped into her mind.

"How was your flight?"

Before she could reply, his brows jerked together. "What have you done to your hair?"

The sudden switch in topic threw Gemma even more off balance. "I needed a change."

He was close enough now that she could see the fine lines fanning out around his eyes, the dark circles beneath, as if lately, like her, he'd been losing sleep.

"And it's not just the hair." His gaze raked over the biscotti suit. He frowned at her glasses. "Since when did you need glasses?"

She drew a breath at his proximity, the sheer energy of his presence, the knowledge that, just days ago, she had woken up in his bed. "Since last week."

Knowledge registered in his gaze. "The story in the press."

The one that very wrongly stated that she had jumped out of Zane's bed, but had unfortunately got it right by saying she had jumped straight into Gabriel's. "I got tired of being a target."

"So this is a disguise?"

"I prefer to call it a reinvention."

His frown deepened. "If you needed protection, you

should have asked me. I could have made sure you got home without being bothered."

Gemma's fingers tightened on the strap of her handbag. "The only reason I get 'bothered' is because of my connection to your family."

"That's regrettably true." Reaching out, he wrapped a finger around a tendril that had escaped the French pleat, his attention once more diverted by her hair. "How long will the brown color last?"

"Sable," she corrected.

The heated patience in his dark eyes told her he didn't care about the shade. "How long?"

For a split second, caught in the blatant possessiveness of the demand, as if he had a right to know intimate details about something as personal as her hair color, she was spun back to the night on Medinos. His intense focus on her then had been utterly seductive—the possessiveness of his touch, the way he'd held her after they had made love, even in sleep, as if he truly hadn't wanted to let her go.

Although that had been a sham. After she had left, Gabriel had not contacted her except in an official capacity, which had proved that their night of passion hadn't really been important to him. "Does it matter?"

"It does to me."

She drew a sharp breath, the proximity of his closeness, his intense focus weaving its spell as her breasts tightened against the fit of her jacket and the slow ache of arousal shimmered to life. Her jaw firmed as she cleared her mind of any crazy romantic illusions. Gabriel's attitude toward her appearance was purely about image. With her appearance toned down, she no doubt didn't quite fit his vision of a fiancée. "Well, it shouldn't."

He shrugged, let the strand of hair go and strolled around behind his desk. "Then I guess we should talk about what's really important. Why did you walk out on me on Medinos?"

She blinked. There it was again—the illusion that he was her lover, that he genuinely cared. "I left a note."

"I read it."

Heart tight in her chest, she rose to her feet, too tense to sit, and found herself staring blindly at the bank of screens flowing with financial data. "I can't have a relationship with you and work for you at the same time."

"But that's exactly what you agreed to do."

She frowned. "We both know I agreed to a pretense, not—"

"Sex."

She threw Gabriel an irritated look, but his face was oddly bland and devoid of emotion. "That's right."

A heavy silence descended on the room. Out in the next office she could hear a phone buzzing, and farther afield she could hear the blare of a car horn, the hum of city traffic. Suddenly Gabriel was close enough that she could feel his heat all down one side.

"You did agree to be my fiancée. We can't do that without touching." To illustrate, he picked up one hand and deliberately threaded his fingers through hers.

A new tension flooded her. She drew a deep breath and tried not to respond. "I've got no problem with appearing to be close in public."

"Good. And you're going to need to dress a little more—" His gaze skimmed the biscotti suit again as if something about it displeased him intensely. He shook his head. "Where did you get that suit?"

She snatched her hand back. "Does it matter?"

"Not really." He had his cell in his hand. He pressed a number to speed dial. A quick conversation later and he hung up. "I've just rung one of the twins, Sophie. She has a designer boutique at the Atraeus Hotel. She should be able to help us."

Gemma blinked at the fact that Gabriel was actually involving a member of his family in the charade. "What do you mean, 'us'?"

His expression was oddly bland. "'Us' as in an engaged couple. We're going shopping."

A brief tap on the door cut through the thickening silence that had followed Gabriel's pronouncement.

Gabriel clamped down on the edgy impatience that, lately, seemed to have become a defining characteristic as Maris walked in with a tray and set it down on the coffee table.

Gemma accepted one of the paper cups that Maris must have sourced from a nearby café as Maris chatted cheerfully. Jaw locked, Gabriel picked up the remaining coffee and stoically waited out the interruption.

Gemma, looking irritatingly unruffled and disarmingly sexy in her secretarial outfit despite the boring color, fielded Maris's superficial questions with a smooth expertise that reminded him that she had been Zane's very competent PA for some years.

As Maris left, he deliberately strolled to the bank of windows that overlooked the street, forcing himself to ease back on the pressure.

Before Gemma had arrived, he had done a standard security check on her. It had been simple enough, given that, courtesy of this temporary position as CEO of Ambrosi Pearls in Auckland, he had access to the Atraeus personnel database.

It shouldn't have been a surprise to find out that she had a degree in performance arts. He could see her creative flare in the scenario with Zane on Medinos and now in this morning's performance.

Finding out that Gemma was trained to act had cast a new light on the impression he had received that she could walk away from him easily. The knowledge that Gemma hadn't slept with anyone since she'd gotten pregnant told him that she didn't give her affections lightly. Put together, those two pieces of information suggested that the fact that he had gotten her back at all was significant.

Cancel significant. He was almost sure that beneath the brisk, professional facade Gemma was still in love with him.

It was the only thing that made sense of her allowing him to make love to her on Medinos.

Every instinct told him that if he messed up now and she walked out, he wouldn't get another chance. On Medinos he had blundered in, locked into his own need and been determined to get his way.

This time, he was determined to keep her close. For a week, maybe longer, he had carte blanche to spoil Gemma, and he intended to do just that.

He finished the coffee and dropped the cup in the trash can beside his desk. He began to outline what would be involved with the temporary engagement. "A week, at least—"

"You said a week on Medinos."

"It could take longer."

There was a small silence as Gemma digested his pronouncement.

Gabriel decided the best tactic was to continue on as if the gray area didn't exist. "Tonight we're having dinner with Mario and Eva. She's a wedding planner—"

Gemma's head came up. "Eva Atraeus? Is she the one your mother and Mario want you to marry?"

Gabriel logged the look of horror on Gemma's face

that his family was lobbying for a marriage between first cousins.

The whole idea was archaic, dynastic, downright Machiavellian in his opinion, and despite the tension amusement tugged at him. "Mario's pushing that one. I think my mother could be looking outside the family."

When Gemma appeared outraged rather than amused, he shrugged and gave up on the joke, although a part of him was loving it that Gemma was mad on his behalf. "Now you're beginning to see what I'm up against," he murmured. "High maintenance doesn't cut it with my family. But, to put your mind at rest, Mario's not trying to sell his daughter into an incestuous marriage. Eva Atraeus isn't a blood relative, she's adopted."

Her gaze flashed. "I'm relieved. If that's the case, I don't know why you didn't ask her—"

"No."

Gemma was silent for a long drawn-out moment, as if trying to gauge whether there was any flexibility in the one short word he'd used. "So why, exactly, do you need to take me shopping?"

Gabriel dragged at his tie, feeling suddenly way out of his depth. "Both Mario and Eva will expect you to be wearing designer clothes and jewelery."

Gabriel frowned as Gemma extracted a small diary and pen from her purse and made a note, as if she was an efficient employee following instructions. "What time is dinner, and where?"

"Eight. I had planned to cater the dinner at my apartment."

She frowned behind the glasses and he had to control the urge to pluck them off the delicate bridge of her nose.

"We're not going out to a restaurant?"

"Not tonight." He watched as she made another small, very efficient note. "Did you want to go out?"

"What I want isn't at issue."

The coolness in her voice informed him that he had made a mistake. It occurred to him, too late, that he had somehow blundered into what his twin sisters, Francesca and Sophie, termed "value" territory. "Mario's old. I didn't want to present him with a fait accompli in a public place."

Instantly, her expression softened and Gabriel found himself relaxing at the hint of approval.

Gemma placed the pen and notebook in her handbag. "What happens if you can't remove Mario as trustee?"

Back on familiar ground, Gabriel propped himself on the edge of his desk. "Mario can't interfere in the day-to-day running of the bank. His power of veto applies to big-ticket investments, which is affecting some of our biggest clients and almost every member of my family. If Nick can't obtain his financing for a big development, he'll have to pull out of the bank and go elsewhere. Both Kyle and Damian have large projects on hold until Mario agrees to release funds." He shrugged. "Their loyalty to me is hurting them."

"So this is hurting your family."

Something relaxed inside of him at Gemma's insight. Family was big with both the Messena and the Atraeus clans, which was the reason he had been reluctant to remove Mario with a psychological evaluation. He was old, but he was family, and until the past six months, he had been an asset. "That's right."

Setting her coffee down, Gemma rose to her feet and walked over to the windows, ostensibly more interested in what was going on down in the street than the tension that vibrated between them. After an interminable few moments, she turned. "Okay. I can do the shopping thing. But I get to choose what I wear."

"Just one proviso. No beige."

Gemma looked faintly disconcerted, as if she'd forgotten their conversation about her new repressed look. "No problem."

Her phone chimed, and Gabriel tensed as she fished her cell out of her bag. The call went through to voice mail and he wondered grimly if it had been Zane she had just ignored, or worse, some other man he didn't know about.

As annoyed as he was, Gabriel didn't make the mistake of pressuring her about the call, sensing that if he pushed too hard she could change her mind about the engagement. "As part of the remuneration package the bank can offer you a loan on any business you want to start."

The quiet way she turned and met his gaze told him that he had just made a further mistake with the offer of finance.

"I don't want a loan, but thank you for offering. All I'll accept is the salary agreed to in the contract I signed and the apartment, since that's part of the remuneration package."

His jaw tightened at her insistence on sticking strictly to the terms of the contract, and the new, quiet distance. In that moment he realized that since Medinos, something had changed. In the few days since she had left his bed, Gemma had become as closed down and crisp as the disguise she was wearing.

He didn't know what, exactly, had changed, but he was determined to find out. "The job itself isn't temporary, just the engagement. The position of PA is real. Maris works for me at the bank. Once Ambrosi Pearls is up and running, and I install a new CEO, she'll come back to the bank with me. Plus there are other positions in the design department and in retail management opening up. With your background with the Atraeus Group, you would be perfect for any one of them."

Her gaze brightened at the possibilities, although he decided he couldn't be sure about what had cheered her up the most: the possibility of her pick of a number of jobs, or the fact that he would soon be leaving.

Gabriel checked his watch and slid his phone out of his pants pocket.

He could sense the conflict that pulled at Gemma, the mystifying factor that constantly saw her applying the brakes to what she so obviously felt for him. But the fact that she had emotions she needed to control was key.

Something shifted inside him, settled.

One week, maybe two.

It wasn't long enough, but it was a start. Despite all the ploys, Gemma did still want him. And when she came back to his bed, like the night on Medinos, he was pretty sure there wouldn't be a lot of conversation involved and that the passion would be the same: searingly hot and mutual.

He punched a speed dial on his phone. The clerk in charge of the bank vault picked up the call. A brief conversation later, and Gabriel set the phone down and extracted his car keys from a desk drawer. "If you'll come with me now, I've arranged to get a ring out of the bank vault, then we'll drop by my sister's shop."

Gemma, in the process of slinging the strap of her handbag over her shoulder, froze. "A ring?"

Gabriel paused at the door, riveted by the combination of uncertainty and pleasure on her face. "I read your P.S. on the note you left in Medinos. Your condition was that we would both have to play our roles to the letter, and in my book that means a ring. Besides, Mario will expect to see one. So will the lawyers."

Before Gemma could argue, he opened the door, which brought Maris into view and earshot.

Pale but composed, Gemma walked past him on a waft of the warm perfume that still had the power to stop him in his tracks. Despite the horrible color, the tight little beige suit was distractingly sexy, and the short skirt made her long legs seem even longer.

His heart slammed against the wall of his chest as he strolled beside Gemma to the elevator. With every moment that passed, he was more and more certain that she cared for him in a deep, meaningful way. It explained the dichotomy of her behavior, the way she'd avoided him at first, but then had melted in his arms.

Relief mingled with a fiery elation coursed through his veins. She hadn't been able to resist him; they hadn't been able to resist each other. He would bring her around. It would take time, but time was a commodity he now possessed.

As he stepped into the elevator with Gemma at his side, a curious feeling swept over him.

For the first time in his life he realized he was approaching a point where he could commit.

Somehow, he had finally ended up in relationship territory.

Eleven

Gemma watched the elevator doors seal shut, closing her in with Gabriel. After spending the night with him, she had realized that she had to tell him about Sanchia. And she intended to do so...when she found the right time.

The fake engagement, as outrageous as it was, would at least give her a few days to find a way to break it to him.

She didn't know how Gabriel would react, or how the situation would work out. All she knew was that Gabriel deserved to know his daughter, and Sanchia needed to know her father. Given that marriage for her was looking doubtful, Gabriel could be the only father Sanchia would ever have. It would be difficult sharing Sanchia, but she knew that ultimately it would be the best thing for her daughter.

The doors swished open. Gabriel's hand cupped her elbow, sending a hot tingle clear up her arm and spinning her back to the night in his apartment.

As they strolled out of the elevator into an underground parking area, she forced herself to relax. For the next week she would have to get used to this kind of casual touching.

Gabriel stopped beside another low-slung muscular car and held the passenger-side door for her. "Did you get custody of your daughter back?"

"Not yet. Getting this job and the apartment sped things up. I should have her back within the week."

Gabriel closed her door and, thankful that he hadn't pushed for more information, Gemma fastened her seat belt.

As he slid into the driver's seat and negotiated the tight lanes of the parking building, she made an effort to relax.

The powerful hum of the car drew her attention as Gabriel accelerated into traffic. Happy to concentrate on anything but personal issues, Gemma examined the interior of what was, she realized, a gorgeous Ferrari. "Somehow I don't see you as a Ferrari kind of guy."

"Tell me, what do you think I should drive?" His gaze briefly connected with hers. His teeth flashed white against his bronzed, clean-shaven jaw, and there they were, back on that dangerous, easy wavelength.

She tried not to respond to the killer smile, the easy charm, and failed. She stared determinedly ahead, concentrating on traffic. "I guess I got used to seeing you in a Jeep Cherokee, like the one you used to drive in Dolphin Bay."

Sunlight flowed into shadow as he pulled into another underground garage. He pulled into a named parking space and turned the powerful engine off. "Maybe that's why I like them."

Feeling suddenly suffocated in the confined space with Gabriel just inches away, his clean male scent keeping her on edge, Gemma busied herself unfastening her seat belt. "Tired of being typecast?"

He shrugged. "When Dad died, overnight I became head of the family, with five siblings, two of them under twenty." He shrugged. "Parenthood at age twenty-five wasn't what I'd planned for my life. Damned if I was going to drive a Volvo or a BMW."

Gemma's fingers curled in on the soft buttery leather of her handbag. Parenthood hadn't been so great at twenty, either. "It's a shock if you're not ready for it."

"Were you?"

The soft question drew her gaze. "By the time I had Sanchia, I was. Now that I'm a mother, I couldn't imagine life without her."

A little annoyed by his probing and the blunt way he was steering the conversation, Gemma asked the one burning question that had kept her awake at night. "Is that why you didn't want any more than the one night we shared six years ago? You wanted to preserve what freedom you had?"

"The business and the family were under a lot of pressure. A relationship wasn't viable."

Even though she hated the answer, it was a reason she understood. Gabriel had had his choices taken away. He had shouldered the burden for his family, even though it had meant putting his own dreams and desires on hold.

Given the sacrifices he'd already had to make, she could understand his distaste for being maneuvered into a marriage not of his choosing.

More than ever, she was happy that she hadn't told him she was pregnant, that she'd chosen to take responsibility for the outcome of that night. For Gabriel, having an instant wife and family forced on him would, literally, have been the last straw.

Gabriel locked the Ferrari then led the way into the bank through a door with a security PIN.

The chill of air-conditioning was a relief after the humid heat, cooling her skin as they strolled through hushed, carpeted corridors, past offices occupied by beautifully suited executives.

Gabriel acknowledged staff as they walked past. When she asked how many people worked for the company, the number of personnel he employed took her breath. The bank was the hub of a financial community, and Gabriel was tasked with overseeing it all.

For the first time she understood the crushing burden taking over all this had been. While she had been struggling with a life-changing pregnancy, Gabriel had been fighting to control all of this.

He opened a door and allowed her to precede him through to an older part of the building possessed of beautiful mosaic floors and soaring ceilings decorated with intricate plaster moldings. Light flooded through high arched windows, imbuing the rooms with a lavish, Italianate glow, and dark paneled doors opened into large offices fitted out with state-of-the art electronics.

She stared at the painstakingly preserved gold leaf embellishing an already ornate ceiling rose, a hand-painted fresco depicting saints and sinners. Whimsically, she decided that with his olive skin and the fierce male beauty of his features, Gabriel could have been an angel lifted straight out of the fresco. And in that moment a part of Gabriel that she had never quite understood fell into place. In all the years she had known him, she had never seen him in his true environment, at the leading edge of a dynasty, and at the center of the Messena empire.

Gabriel didn't attempt to take her arm again, for which she was grateful, because she was still coming to terms with this new view of him and a whole host of contrary emotions.

Disappointment and regret, a crazy longing to follow up on the cues he was giving her and claim the ephemeral closeness of a temporary relationship, even if it meant she was going to be badly hurt.

Gabriel lifted a hand to a burly man dressed in a security uniform who had just stepped out of a side room. Minutes later, they were taken through another security door and shown through to the section of the vault given over to safe-deposit boxes.

Gemma shivered slightly at the cooler temperature as Gabriel extracted a box, set it on a table and waited for the guard to insert his key. He then produced his own to unlock the box. Inside there were a number of jewelry cases stacked one on another. He chose a case marked with a symbol that Gemma, through her years of working for the Atraeus family, recognized instantly.

She stiffened. "You can't give me that. It's Fabergé."

She looked around quickly, to make sure the security guard hadn't overheard, but he had already retreated to a small glassed-in office.

"As my fiancée you would be expected to wear significant jewelry. This set belonged to my great-grandmother Eugenie. She was Russian."

Gabriel flipped open the box. Inside was a gorgeous set, which included a diamond necklace, earrings, a gorgeous set of hair clips and a ring. The diamonds were large and shimmered with burning flashes of fire under the lights, signaling purity and perfection of cut. She couldn't imagine the cost of the diamonds, let alone the fact that they were designed and set by Fabergé.

Gemma shook her head. "No. Absolutely not."

"It's either this, or we have to go to a jewelry store in town." He checked his watch. "We're due at Sophie's shop in half an hour. If you want to shop for something else, we can do that afterward."

Gemma sent Gabriel a frustrated look. "There's no point in shopping for a ring when I only need it for a few days."

"Then wear this." Gabriel picked the ring out and insisted she try it on. "You need a ring for tonight. If this one fits, we'll take it."

"We could get a piece of costume jewelry, or else something smaller and cheaper—"

Gabriel's glance cut her off. "No Messena bride would wear anything but family jewels—it's tradition. Mario is a traditionalist to the bone. He'll want to see which set you've been given." The faint ruefulness of his glance softened the demand.

"There must be something smaller and cheaper in the box—"

"If there was, no Messena bride would wear it."

Despite herself the phrase *Messena bride* sent a small thrill through her. "I'm not a bride, not even close."

"And that's not even close to an excuse." Picking up her left hand, Gabriel slipped the ring on her third finger.

The warmth of his fingers, the faint calloused roughness against her skin sent another sharp little kick of sensation through her. The ring warmed against her skin. Her breath caught; the fit was perfect.

Gemma lifted her head, which was a mistake, because Gabriel was so close. Her gaze caught and held with his and for a long, drawn-out moment she thought he might kiss her.

She blinked, unexpectedly emotional, because the ring, this scene, was something she had never dared dream about. Yet here she was, and Gabriel had just placed the most beautiful engagement ring she had ever seen on her finger. It should have meant fidelity and undying love; instead it meant absolutely nothing.

The sharp little pang of hurt finally made her face something she should have known all along. She wasn't just fatally attracted to Gabriel; somehow, despite all of the things that had gone wrong between them, she was in love with him. Seriously, devastatingly, in love.

She felt the blood drain from her face. Straight-out warmth and friendship she could cope with, but she knew the extremity of her nature. It had gotten her into trouble often enough. Issues were black or white, emotions either hot or cold. If she was in love, that was it.

Gabriel's hands closed around her upper arms, steadying her. "Are you all right? You went dead white just then."

"I'm fine. A little tired." Even though she knew she would be compounding the situation by letting him touch her, she allowed him to draw her close. For a few moments she gloried in the anchoring heat of his touch, his concern, and examined the frightening truth: that even fighting and arguing, she would rather be with Gabriel than anyone.

She loved being with him now, touching him, wrapped in his warmth, the beat of his heart thudding in her ear. She loved him, and it couldn't be.

Misery wound through her. In that moment she recognized a stark truth. As much as she wanted to marry and settle down, to have a husband she could love and more children, it wasn't going to happen.

She wasn't going to fall for anyone else. She had been in love with Gabriel for years. If she was honest, since she was about sixteen years old and had volunteered to help her father at the Messena estate, just so she could catch a glimpse of Gabriel.

It explained how curiously content she had been not to

date or get involved with any of the men who had tried to entice her into relationships after she had gotten pregnant.

Loosening his hold, she sniffed, still ridiculously emotional. She glanced at the ring, which burned with an impossibly white fire, desperate for a distraction, because any moment now she was going to cry.

Surreptitiously, she dashed at one dampening tear, but the movement alerted Gabriel, who was busy repacking the safe-deposit box.

"Hey." He cupped her face and brushed his thumbs over her cheeks and pulled her close.

She stiffened for a moment, then gave in, wound her arms around his waist and leaned into him. Distantly, she registered the firmness of his arousal, although the hug was devoid of sexual demand. Gabriel just seemed content to hold her.

A sound from the small glass office made her stiffen.

The moment broken, Gabriel let her go. Automatically, she started to tug the ring off.

"Leave it on," Gabriel said quietly. "That's the whole point."

The security guard collected the box and as he did so he glanced at the ring. "Just got engaged?"

He beamed, his face pink as he shook hands with Gabriel. "I tried not to notice, Mr. Messena, but I couldn't help but see that something special was happening. Have you named the date?"

Gemma opened her mouth to protest, but a dark glance from Gabriel cut her short. "We haven't set a date yet."

Gabriel introduced her to the guard, Evan. When he heard her name, he frowned. "The name's familiar."

Gemma's stomach sank, but Gabriel forestalled any further questions by picking up the case that contained the rest of the jewels, slipping them in his jacket pocket then checking his watch again.

After asking after Evan's wife, who apparently suffered from arthritis, and successfully diverting him, Gabriel urged her from the room, one hand at the small of her back.

Gemma caught the reflected glitter of the diamond on her finger as the heavy vault door swung closed behind them. Another set of doors, these ones made of heavy glass, threw their reflection back at them.

Gabriel looked tall, broad-shouldered and darkly handsome; Gemma looked unexpectedly voluptuous and Italian in the biscotti suit. By some kind of weird alchemy the color had added a richness to her hair and invested her pale skin with an olive glow. With the flash of the diamond on her finger, she looked every bit the expensive, pampered bride.

As they turned a corner into the mosaic floors and gorgeous architecture of the lavish office suites, Gabriel indicated that he needed to collect something from his office.

He smiled as Gemma looked curiously around the light-flooded room. "One of the perks of the job. If you want to freshen up, there's a bathroom through there."

Bemused, Gemma checked out the cream marbled bathroom, which contained a walk-in shower and a heated towel rail draped with fluffy white towels. She was used to the Atraeus family and their extreme wealth, so she was accustomed to opulent surroundings. She guessed she just wasn't used to seeing Gabriel in the center of the same kind of elaborate wealth and power. In Dolphin Bay he had seemed attainable. Here he did not.

As she stepped back out into Gabriel's office and his gaze connected with hers, the tension she had briefly managed to leave behind returned full force.

While he checked his computer, she sank into a leather

chair that felt like a cloud and tried not to fall in love with the ring on her finger, or the shattering, improbable idea that Gabriel might want the engagement to be real.

Even if Gabriel did genuinely want her, the second he found out about Sanchia, everything would change. He wouldn't be happy that she had kept Sanchia from him and they would be forever linked in a way that took away his choice. There would be no more easy companionship or heart-pounding lovemaking. Nothing would be either simple or easy between them again.

A quick tap at the door and a husky female voice had her head turning. A pretty, blue-eyed brunette came in, a sleek computer tablet in one hand. Dressed in an elegant white suit that made her skin look like porcelain, and possessed of a delicate serene beauty, for a confused moment Gemma thought she was Lilah Cole, then the differences registered. Her hair was shorter, just brushing her shoulders in a sleek bob, and she was shorter and more delicately built.

Not tall and just a little lanky, or too forthright, as Gemma was.

Gabriel made introductions, but before Gemma could do more than acknowledge Simone, apparently one of the bank's investment analysts, Gabriel walked her out into the corridor, where he completed his discussion with her.

As the conversation ended, Simone glanced in the door and gave Gemma a long, silent look before turning on her heel and strolling back to wherever it was she had come from.

Gemma realized that somewhere along the way she had forgotten to breathe. As Gabriel collected a briefcase from his desk, she rose to her feet. The glitter of the gorgeous ring caught her eye again, and she wished, too late, that she hadn't hidden it in her lap while Simone was in the room.

Finally, she identified the emotion twisting in her stomach. Picking up her handbag, she waited for Gabriel and
wondered if she could find something solid she could bang
her head against.

If she'd had any doubts about the in-love diagnosis they
were gone. After all of the progress she'd made in walking
away from Gabriel and trying to neutralize the irresistible
attraction, she had somehow managed to progress another
step in the wrong direction.

She was fiercely, primitively jealous.

Twelve

Gemma dressed for the evening in a slinky tangerine gown Gabriel's sister Sophie had helped her choose. Gabriel arrived, still dressed in the suit he'd worn to the office, to pick her up, but insisted on coming in for a moment.

Reluctant to allow him in because the place was dotted with photographs of Sanchia, and the odd toy, she agreed, then rushed around, jamming photos and toys in cupboards.

She left one photograph of Sanchia as a chubby baby out, because it would be strange if she didn't have any. Even that was a risk, because with her dark hair and eyes Sanchia looked heart-stoppingly like a Messena.

When Gabriel stepped inside her apartment, she logged his instant, searing appreciation and felt suddenly self-conscious. The tangerine dress was much more her natural style—bright and pretty with an edge of sophistication. But after seeing Simone in his office, with her subtle, perfectly cut clothes and serene beauty, she wondered a little desperately what Gabriel found attractive about her.

He slipped the Fabergé case out of his pocket and extracted the diamond necklace. "I want you to wear this tonight, as well."

Gemma stared at the cascade of diamonds shooting off fiery sparks under her lights. "Because Mario will expect it."

Gabriel's gaze was abruptly soft enough to make her heart melt. "No. Because I'd like you to wear them."

"That is not a good answer."

"It's the truth."

She drew a breath and turned, lifting the weight of her hair away from her neck.

The oval mirror in the hall framed Gabriel as he fastened the necklace at her nape. She fingered the diamonds where they warmed against her skin. The pure, fiery light of the jewels was a perfect foil for the dress. "They look beautiful." Although almost all of her attention was on his hands where they cupped her bare shoulders.

"They suit you."

Taking a deep breath, she smiled brightly. "Diamonds suit anyone."

She moved away from his touch before she did something sillier, like turning into his arms and kissing him. Instead, she picked up her evening bag and the wrap, which was neatly folded on the small table in the hall.

Gabriel paused beside the small table beneath the mirror. "Is this a picture of Sanchia?"

Her heart banged against the wall of her chest as she saw Gabriel with the baby photo in his hands. "Yes."

A small silence formed as he replaced the frame on the table. Feeling worse than she had expected to feel, Gemma opened the door and pointedly waited.

Gabriel's gaze was enigmatic as he walked out onto her front porch, and she wondered a little anxiously if he'd seen any resemblance to photos of other Messena babies.

Gabriel held the car door for her then walked around and climbed into the driver's seat. As he accelerated away she sent him a fleeting glance. "So who's cooking tonight?"

"If you're asking me if I can cook, I can, but it's strictly survival stuff. Maris rang a local restaurant that caters dinner parties. They're delivering."

Warmed by the relaxed timbre of his voice, the way that he loosened off his tie as he drove, as if he was unwinding from the day's work, Gemma looked away from the clean lines of his profile and tried to focus instead on the neon signs and illuminated shop windows of downtown Auckland.

Gabriel ran the gamut of Queen Street and the series of traffic lights then turned along the waterfront. Eventually, he turned into a gated apartment complex in Mission Bay.

Opening the front door of an apartment that was the size of a small mansion, with ground-floor access and three stories, he allowed her to precede him into the hall then on into a large lounge with a towering ceiling. He checked his watch. "I need to shower and change before Mario and Eva get here. Make yourself at home."

He showed her the kitchen and formal dining room and invited her to help herself to the trays of drinks and nibbles the caterers had left out.

Setting her evening bag and wrap down on one of the stools that were grouped along the kitchen bar, Gemma decided to familiarize herself with the apartment before Eva and Mario arrived. Since she was supposed to be Gabriel's fiancée, it would look a little strange if she didn't even know where the bathroom was.

Gabriel had gone upstairs, so she figured it was safe

enough to open doors downstairs. On her second try she found a small gleaming bathroom. As she closed the door, the front doorbell buzzed.

Adrenaline arrowed through her veins as she walked to the door and opened it. She wasn't ready; she hadn't had time to look through kitchen cupboards or work out the stereo, but it was too late now. When she opened the door, an ultrasexy and quite lovely brunette stepped inside, carrying a frosted bottle of champagne.

A small frown pleated her brow when she saw Gemma. "Hello. Are you a friend of Gabriel's?"

Gemma took a deep breath. "Actually, I'm his fiancée."

Shock registered in her gaze. Her eyes dropped to Gemma's left hand. "He gave you the Fabergé."

When she didn't say anything more, Gemma calmly asked if there was anyone else to come in. When Eva indicated there wasn't, that her father was arriving later, she closed the door. "Gabriel's, uh, just in the shower. Come through and I'll get you a drink."

That was, if she could find the glasses.

Eva strolled to the kitchen, not waiting for Gemma. "How long have you known Gabriel?"

Gemma almost gave a sigh of relief. At least this part was easy enough. "Years. Most of my life, actually."

"Then you must be from Dolphin Bay."

Gemma began opening cupboard doors, looking for glasses. "Yes."

Eva frowned, somehow managing to look even more gorgeous. "You look familiar. Maybe I've seen you at a family gathering?"

Gemma pretended not to hear that one. Finally, she found wineglasses and set them on the counter. When she picked up the bottle of wine, thankfully it had a screw top so she didn't have to search for a corkscrew.

Eva took the glass of wine she poured and walked into the lounge to stare out at the view. "If you were at Constantine's wedding, maybe I saw you there."

Gemma studied the taut expression of Eva's face, the combative stance. "I wasn't at Constantine's wedding."

"But you know him?"

"Yes, I do." Gemma bit her tongue against the urge to supply more information, just in case Eva guessed who she really was.

Feeling stressed, and wishing Gabriel would hurry up and come down, she bypassed the wine and poured herself a glass of water instead. The way the night was going, she was going to have to keep her wits about her.

Eva returned to the kitchen counter and set her glass of wine down. "I hope you don't mind if I put on some music? Gabriel's got a great collection of jazz."

Gemma tried for her best neutral smile, the one she used to soothe prickly clients. "Be my guest."

As soon as Eva disappeared into another smaller lounge, evidently the place where the stereo system was to be found, Gemma started up the stairs. As she reached the top, Gabriel stepped out of the shower, a snowy white towel wrapped around his waist. "Eva and Mario are here?"

Loud music began to play. Gemma raised her voice. "Just Eva and a bottle of champagne. Apparently Mario's coming later."

He dragged the fingers of one hand through his damp hair. "Champagne? Damn, there must be something in the air."

Eva's voice drifted up from the bottom of the stairs, her face vivid and engaging. "Dad's got a meeting. He'll be here in half an hour." She frowned. "Gabriel...you didn't tell me you were getting engaged."

"It's only just happened," he said smoothly, and pulled Gemma close.

Her hands skidded over his damp abdomen as she found herself plastered against his side. His arm came around her, clamping her tight against him. Before she could protest, Gabriel dropped a light kiss on her mouth, then she was free.

If the drinks were difficult, dinner was worse.

Mario, an impeccably dressed older man, arrived with one of Gabriel's younger brothers. Kyle, like all of the Messena men, was tall and dark, with a sleekly muscular frame. Although instead of dark eyes, his were a cool, piercing shade of green. A short haircut and a tough jaw completed a look that was more than a shade dangerous and didn't reflect what he did for a living, which was investment banking.

As soon as Kyle saw her, he raised a brow. "Gemma. It's been a long time. The last time I saw you was in Sydney, at some art auction with Zane."

Eva paused in the motion of pouring a glass of champagne for Mario. She looked curious rather than annoyed, for which Gemma was grateful. However much Mario was pushing for a marriage between Gabriel and Eva, evidently Eva hadn't been over the moon about the idea, either.

She continued pouring champagne, although ever since Kyle had stepped into the room her manner had grown even more acerbic. "You didn't say you knew Zane."

"I'm from Dolphin Bay." Gemma looked around a little desperately for Gabriel. "I know them all—Constantine, Lucas, Zane—"

Eva frowned. "I can't remember Zane ever going to Dolphin Bay."

Gabriel, dressed in black trousers and a black gauzy

shirt casually open at the throat, intervened with a cool glance. "He came once, when he was fourteen or fifteen, before he went away to college."

Gemma breathed a sigh of relief and sent Gabriel a thankful glance. She guessed it didn't really matter if Eva found out that she was Zane's notorious ex-PA. If there had been a problem, Gabriel would never have asked her to pose as his fiancée in the first place.

Gabriel shook Mario's hand and formally introduced Gemma.

Mario's gaze was glacial, but he was polite. When he noticed the ring he met Gabriel's gaze for a long moment then inclined his head. "That's a very beautiful ring," he said with something like resignation. "Congratulations."

Mario turned to Eva with a frown. "You could have been wearing that ring!"

"Dad!" Eva sent him a reproving glance then rolled her eyes at Gabriel. "Sorry, Gabriel. Dad just could never accept that we aren't destined to be together."

Mario's reproving gaze was directed firmly at Eva. "You need a husband."

Eva smiled, although there was a definite edge to it as she poured herself another glass of champagne. "I'm wedded to my business."

Mario shrugged and sat down. "Women," he said repressively, "shouldn't be in business."

There was a tiny, vibrating silence, then Kyle jumped in to break it by taking Gemma's hand and studying the ring.

He sent Gabriel a curious look. "Great rock. Very historical."

Gabriel handed him a beer. "You're here to run interference," he murmured, "not start a fight."

Kyle released Gemma's hand and grinned. "Gotcha. Guess I'll go sit by Eva. That'll be fun."

Gabriel's hand landed in the small of Gemma's back, the warmth of his palm burning through the silk. A now familiar tingling heat shivered through Gemma. "Do you think it's safe to eat?"

"As long as we hand out plastic knives."

She glanced at her ring. "What is it with this ring? Everyone seems to recognize it."

"Which is exactly why I chose it." Gabriel went into the kitchen and opened a huge stainless-steel oven, where covered dishes were keeping warm. "It has a bit of history attached to it. Eugenie had a reputation for being elusive. My great-grandfather wooed her across two continents. She finally succumbed when he produced the jewels."

Gemma would have liked to know more, because the story sounded enchanting, but Gabriel was unloading hot dishes onto heat pads, so she grabbed a set of oven mitts and started carrying dishes to the table. It was a Mediterranean-style feast, with a platter of dips and antipasto and deliciously fragrant savory pastries.

Gabriel pulled out her chair at the table and poured wine. Mario said grace in his native Medinian, his voice soft and cracked with age.

The first course was rocky. Mario's conversation was stilted, and it was clear that at times he was having trouble remembering things. Eva seemed intent on drawing out more about just how and when Gabriel had proposed and when the wedding was.

It was a relief to get up from the table, help clear plates away and serve up the rich beef stew that had been sitting in a chafing dish, along with rice, spicy lentils and a green salad. By the time they reached dessert, a rich tiramisu, Eva had stopped asking questions. Gemma was uneasily certain, owing to the measuring glances that Eva kept sending her way, that despite the change in hair color she had finally realized who Gemma was.

Gabriel picked up on her unease and sent Kyle a steady look that was some kind of signal. Kyle immediately got up and offered to drive both Eva and Mario home. Mario had arrived by taxi and Eva had driven, but because Eva had had two glasses of wine, Kyle refused to let her drive.

As soon as they were gone, Gemma let out a sigh of relief and helped Gabriel clear up and fill the dishwasher. While she did that, he loaded all of the chafing dishes and large serving platters into a large box for the caterer to collect. When the kitchen was clean, she collected her wrap and bag.

Gabriel met her gaze, his own oddly somber and guarded, and she caught the subtext. She could stay if she wanted.

Despite the small amount of wine she'd sipped through dinner, she had managed to stay sober for the express purpose of avoiding moments like this. "I can get a taxi back to the apartment."

Gabriel frowned. "I'll drive you home."

The drive home was quiet, the streets mostly empty. When Gabriel braked for lights, Gemma studied his profile and tried not to remember the pulse-pounding kiss. "Did the dinner achieve what you wanted?"

His gaze touched on hers. "Mario knows his trusteeship is coming to an end. I spoke to him before he left. We have a meeting with the law firm in the morning."

"Then the legal situation should be wrapped up inside a week."

"It's possible."

He accelerated through the lights and pulled over into her street. Instead of staying in the car, he insisted on seeing her to her apartment. When she paused at her door, he took the key from her hand, unlocked the door and insisted on seeing her into the apartment itself.

When Gemma saw the baby picture of Sanchia, she thought again about telling Gabriel that he had a daughter, but he walked past the photo and the moment passed.

She set her evening bag and wrap down, suddenly on tenterhooks even more than she had been in his house. Somehow it seemed unbearably intimate to have Gabriel in her small apartment, with her bedroom just visible down the hall. "So, what else do we have to do with this charade?"

His movements deliberate, he linked his fingers with hers and drew her close. "This." Bending close, he touched his mouth to hers.

When he lifted his head, his gaze was dark and intense. "And maybe we could talk about the real reason you walked away from what we had in Medinos."

She closed her eyes, melting inside. "I didn't think you seriously wanted anything more."

He cupped her neck, his thumbs smoothing along her jaw. "It's been a long time, but I've never forgotten you. When we were on Medinos I realized I shouldn't have let you go all those years ago. Babe, I want you back."

The words, the husky endearment, shivered through her. For a split second she was unable to absorb the concept. Not when she had been engraving the exact opposite message on her brain for six years.

He kissed her again, this time taking his time.

He wanted her back.

A crazy, dizzying elation shimmered through her.

Underneath all of the reasons that she shouldn't make love with Gabriel again—number one being that she hadn't told him about Sanchia—she was completely, utterly seduced. All evening he had been attentive. Fake engagement or not, he had put that beautiful ring on her finger and she had felt like his fiancée.

She pulled back. "Why do you want me when we haven't seen each other for six years? It doesn't make sense."

"You're beautiful. I've always liked you. This is why." Cupping her face, he brushed his mouth across hers. The caress shuddered through her, evoking memories she thought she had buried, swamping her with emotions that were at once intense and painful and yet unbearably sweet.

One more night. What could it hurt?

Despite all the reasons to say no, temptation pulled at her.

A few more days and everything would change, because he would know about Sanchia.

Her stomach hollowed out. Once he found out she would never experience this again, the passionate highs and the desperate lows. And in that moment the decision was made.

One more night. She would tell him about Sanchia in the morning.

Lifting up, she wound her arms around his neck. "I want you, too, but you've always known that."

She kissed him back and his arms closed around her. She found herself being slowly walked back until they were in her room. He unzipped her dress. It puddled on the floor as she unfastened his shirt, fingers slipping on the small buttons in her haste.

He shrugged out of the shirt. The street lighting from outside shafted through her window shutters, tiger-striping his body with dim gold and inky shadow. As he unhooked her bra and took one breast into his mouth, she was spun back to the dark room on Medinos, the storm pounding on the windows.

Another step and he pulled her down onto the bed with

him. Gabriel eased out of his trousers then peeled her panties off in one smooth movement and they were both naked. "You're beautiful," he said softly.

Seconds later, he rejoined her on the bed. The next kiss tingled all the way to her toes. Groaning, Gabriel rolled, pulling her beneath him. Gemma wound her arms around his neck and pulled him closer still. Another kiss, and then there was no more need for words.

Thirteen

Gabriel came out of sleep as the first slivers of dawn light flowed through the shutters, aware instantly that Gemma was with him.

Broodingly, he turned on his side and simply watched her.

Despite the lovemaking there was something wrong, something he couldn't quite put his finger on. He would find out what was creating the cool distance and do what he could to eliminate the problem. It would take time, but he had plenty of that.

Now that he had her back in his bed, he didn't intend to rush things.

A sense of satisfaction filled him that she had his ring on his finger. In a day or two, he would suggest they make the engagement real. Maybe it was a bit early, but he couldn't see the point in waiting now.

He noticed the dark shadows beneath Gemma's eyes

and decided that now they were engaged, even if she saw it only as a fake engagement, he would intervene with the department that was giving her a problem with custody.

Gemma must have been worried sick about her small daughter, but all of that would end now. He would take care of her. As his fiancée she would be cushioned and cared for, and there would be no more financial hardship.

If she would accept the help.

The O'Neills were fiercely proud and independent. In their own way, just as stiff-necked and proud as his own family.

Despite the pretty clothes and the social veneer she had learned as Zane's PA, Gemma was an O'Neill through and through.

His decision to make the engagement real solidified. He had dated enough women to know that Gemma was different in a way that mattered.

Aside from the searing attraction, he liked her and he was no longer worried that the passion that bound them together was the obsessive kind that could prove destructive. The trouble he'd had getting Gemma back into his bed had proved that.

The ring on her finger glimmered in the morning light. The diamond was breathtakingly valuable, with a notable history. If he should ever choose to sell it there was a list of buyers registered at Sotheby's, one of them prepared to buy at any cost. Getting the ring from the vault was a significant move, which Eva, Kyle and Mario had recognized.

The fact that he had put that particular ring on Gemma's finger signaled that Gabriel was prepared to undertake a situation that was not entered into lightly by any Messena.

Marriage.

* * *

The flowers arrived later on in the morning as Gemma dressed for the meeting with Mario and the lawyers who dealt with the trust.

She wrapped herself in a robe and collected the enormous bunch of pink roses from the courier, then set about trying to find vases. She had just filled every container she had when a second delivery, this time of rich, deep red roses, arrived.

Dizzy with delight that Gabriel had thought to send flowers, she searched out jars and jugs from kitchen cupboards. She set containers of flowers around the apartment, on every available surface, and took a moment to breathe in the perfume before she had to dash back to her room and finish dressing.

An emerald-green silk dress with a sleek black jacket over top, which she had gotten from Sophie Messena's boutique, produced a look that was both stunningly feminine and businesslike.

After coiling her hair up in a loose, sexy knot, she dabbed on perfume and slipped into a pair of high heels. With the diamond on her finger, she looked and felt like the pampered, expensive bride-to-be of a very rich man.

She heard the throaty roar of the Ferrari and her stomach clenched on a jolt of pure, 100 percent in-love emotion. She was so happy she could cry, but at the same time she was aware that she was living in a fool's paradise.

Gabriel, who had left earlier to go back to his apartment and shower and change before coming back to pick her up, was parked out on the street. As Gemma walked out of the front door of her apartment block to meet him, he held the passenger-side door open for her.

Gemma couldn't stop smiling. "I got the flowers."

"Good." Pulling her loosely into his arms, he kissed her.

Long seconds later, Gemma slid into her seat and watched Gabriel as he strolled around the bonnet of the car. In that moment she was almost terrifyingly happy and content.

A short drive downtown and they walked into an expansive, leather-scented office. Don Cade, a lawyer who looked to be of the same vintage as Mario, got to his feet. While Mario appeared a little vague at times, Cade was as sharp as a rapier.

He eyed her ring as he shook her hand, his perusal discreet but thorough. Gabriel pulled out a chair for her next to his own, and the proceedings began.

A second, younger man entered the room and was introduced as Holloway, an associate of the firm.

Gabriel frowned at Holloway, and minutes later, when he began producing newspaper clippings and other evidence that proved that Gemma could not seriously be Gabriel's real fiancée, Gemma realized why.

Holloway was a private detective.

Cade directed all of his comments to Gabriel, completely ignoring Gemma, and she realized he had known all of the information that had been presented before he had met her. The gist of it was that Cade was erring on the side of retaining Mario's trusteeship. Gemma decided it was a setup if she had ever seen one.

Annoyed beyond belief, she found herself on her feet, confronting the lawyer directly. "The evidence you've amassed to prove there isn't an engagement is impressive, but unfortunately, your man didn't dig deep enough." She directed a scathing glance at Holloway. "Any investigator worth their salt would never rely on tabloid and internet reports, which are all lies anyway."

She ignored the surprised cough from Holloway and

ploughed on. "You're saying we're not engaged, but it didn't feel like that last night. In bed."

Cade frowned. Holloway opened his mouth to say something, but Gabriel cut him down with a glance.

Gabriel switched his icy gaze to Cade. "I suggest, if you want to retain my business, that you ask your man to leave now."

Cade turned to Holloway and advised him to go in a low tone, but Gemma noticed that Holloway left his report on the table.

Cade picked up the report and began intoning his verdict in a low voice.

Incensed, Gemma reached into her purse and extracted Sanchia's passport, which her sister had posted to her along with some other correspondence just the previous day. "If you think Gabriel and I don't have a real relationship, you're wrong." Her stomach twisted sickly at what she had to do, but there was no way past it.

Opening Sanchia's passport, she slapped it down in front of Cade. "Gabriel and I have a daughter. She's five years old. I think that's a bit more believable than a tabloid exclusive from a reporter named Lucky Starr."

She turned to Gabriel, barely able to meet his gaze. "I'm sorry."

Picking up Holloway's report, she ripped it into pieces, tossed it on Cade's desk and walked out.

Gabriel arrived at Gemma's apartment minutes later, Sanchia's passport in his pocket. He knew Gemma was here because he had followed her as she'd run out of Cade's offices and hailed a taxi. Keeping close to the taxi across town had been difficult because he'd gotten caught at a set of lights, but it hadn't taken long to guess her destination.

He buzzed her apartment, half expecting that she wouldn't let him in, but she did almost immediately.

The first thing he noticed when he walked into Gemma's lounge was a suitcase filled with brightly colored articles of clothing, which Gemma had placed on one armchair. Drawn by the intensely feminine pale pink fabric, he pulled the top item of clothing out...and went still inside.

His fingers closed on silk and tulle. He sat down on an adjacent seat, his heart pounding.

The tutu, because that's what it was, was somehow more real than the passport photo had been, because it was a practical object. Clothing for his child.

He took a deep breath, pinched the bridge of his nose.

Now it all made sense: Gemma avoiding him over the years. There was no other explanation as to why they hadn't bumped into each other.

No matter how often he had gone to Atraeus social events in Sydney, despite the fact that Gemma was part of the firm, she had never been present while he had been there.

Gemma sat down opposite him. "I was going to tell you."

"When, exactly?"

"Today. I just wanted one more night before you found out." She sat down in the armchair opposite him, gorgeous in the green dress, her face pale.

"What did you think I would do?" he said flatly. "Finish with you?"

Her expression was pale but composed. "Yes."

Like he had done six years ago.

He drew a deep breath, let it out slowly, his mind racing—a far cry from his usual disciplined process. "I'm not going to. We need to get married. It should have happened years ago." He stopped and remembered to breathe again. "Can I see a photo of her?"

Without answering, Gemma walked across to a sideboard and opened a cupboard. A mass of frames tumbled out, and suddenly the extent of the deception hurt.

Gemma had hidden the photos, hidden his daughter from him.

As Gemma collected the frames in a stack, her fingers quick and just a little clumsy, she knocked the top one and they all cascaded across the floor.

Gabriel moved before he could think, helping her pick up the quirky catalog of Sanchia: the chubby baby, the cheerful little girl with dark eyes and hair like his and the same lanky grace as her mother.

The colors of the frames were just as bright and whimsical as Gemma's clothes, pink and yellow, blue and green—candy colors sprinkled with a liberal amount of bling.

Gabriel's heart squeezed in his chest as he drank in the images and fell utterly in love with his daughter. It hit him just how much of Sanchia's life he had missed. Although as knee-jerk as that reaction was, he knew he couldn't afford to dwell on it.

The years at the bank and dealing with his volatile family had taught him the danger of allowing emotion to rule. He had a daughter—now, today.

He stared at a photo of Sanchia, a birthday hat jammed on her head, a smear of chocolate on one cheek, grinning straight at him. A perilous joy gripped his heart. No matter what, he couldn't afford to mess this up.

Gemma handed him a pink folder, flipped open to show a series of photos of Sanchia as a newborn, tiny and serene, all red skin and damp dark hair and wrapped in white. "When you rang to ask me if I was pregnant, I didn't think I was. I had periods until I was three months along and by then I was back at university, busy with exams. It didn't register that something was wrong until I reached four months."

Gemma indicated the first photo. "Sanchia was about five minutes old there. My sister took the photos."

Gabriel studied the tiny, exquisite baby, Gemma pale and exhausted as she held her. "Your sister was with you at the birth?"

"Yes. No one else." Her gaze connected bleakly with his. "There's been no one else. No other man."

For a long, drawn-out moment, Gabriel forgot the photos, his chest tightening as he absorbed the stunning fact that Gemma had only ever been his. "So why didn't you tell me you were pregnant? We could have gotten married."

"I didn't think that would happen."

He was silent for a moment. "You're right. After what happened with Dad my hands were tied. Damn, this is a mess."

"Apart from the fact that I knew you were busy with your family and the business, I thought that if you really did want me, you wouldn't be able to stay away from me, but you did. Completely. Not even a phone call." She sat back on her knees, creating a subtle distance. "I was in the same city as you, studying. You knew that. Some days I actually walked past the Messena building, trying to catch a glimpse of you. A couple of times I even saw you."

"You should have contacted me—"

"So you could come and see that I was pregnant?"

Her fierce frown told him how repugnant that idea had been to her. He shrugged. "We would have sorted something out—"

"Sorry. I didn't want charity." She gave him a quick neutral smile, the inner toughness he had always admired suddenly surfacing. "I could see why I was completely not what you wanted in a wife."

In that moment any uncertainty about Gemma's feelings for him evaporated. "You loved me."

"For a long time." Her expression was self-effacing. "Why else do you think I was so keen to help Dad with the gardens at your place? Why I slept with you?" Jerkily, she rose to her feet, gathered the frames and placed them on the coffee table as if she couldn't bear to talk about it any longer.

Grimly, Gabriel rose to his feet. Gemma's white face, her uncharacteristic clumsiness, hit him forcibly.

He needed time; they both needed time, but in that moment he knew he couldn't afford to give Gemma that kind of space. The minute he eased back, she would close him out.

He placed the folder of Sanchia's first hours on the coffee table. "I meant what I said about getting married, so what do you think about making the engagement real?"

Fourteen

Gemma unlocked her arms from around her waist and watched as Gabriel rose to his feet. With his dark gaze leveled at her, she felt exposed and vulnerable. Gabriel knew that he was the only one, that she loved him. She had no defenses left.

Pure white fire glinted off the engagement ring, reminding her of something else she didn't have: his love.

Gabriel wanted to marry her, but essentially she was still the same person she'd been when he hadn't wanted her in his life.

The things that had changed were all external. They shared a child, and marriage, even to someone like her, would help him solidify his hold on his family's company.

It wasn't the true, deep love, the fairy-tale relationship, she had always wanted. Gabriel was offering a practical solution. "You don't have to marry me, but if you want to go ahead with a wedding, then I accept. I've already told Sanchia about you, and she wants you in her life. She can't wait to meet you."

They reached Dolphin Bay at four in the afternoon. Gabriel drove straight to Lauren's house, which was situated in a little suburb one street away from the beach.

He parked the Ferrari out on the street. Gemma fumbled free of her seat belt and pushed her door open, her heart swelling with the straightforward joy of homecoming and the fact that any second now, Sanchia would burst out of the door.

The salt tang of the air hit her face. As she hitched her handbag over one shoulder, Gemma noticed a bunch of kids across the road openly staring at the vehicle.

Gabriel had already grabbed her suitcase of gifts out from behind the seats, along with a package of his own. As he straightened, expression remote behind a pair of dark glasses, he lifted a hand at the boys then glanced at her. "Aren't those the Roberts kids?"

Gemma reached into her bag and found her sunglasses. "How did you know that?"

He walked around the bonnet, looking more casual and sexy than she could ever remember in faded, glove-soft jeans and a white V-neck T-shirt that clung across his chest. "Their mother used to teach the twins piano after school. Her kids used to come over and swim in the pool. Pretty sure I recognized some of those faces."

He held the front gate to a weatherboard house with bikes and assorted toys littering the front yard. As he did, the front door was flung open and a small, dark whirlwind burst out.

Gemma braced herself for the impact and wrapped Sanchia in her arms, soaking in the feel and smell of her, tears squeezing past her lids. Yesterday she had gotten the all-clear from the welfare department, but the relief of that was now tempered with this new situation.

Sanchia pulled free and turned her attention to Gabriel. Her likeness to Gabriel was acute, even down to the quiet, assessing way she regarded him before speaking, a trait that was Gabriel's own.

She frowned, her gaze intense. "Are you the dad?"

Gabriel dropped down on his haunches. Even so, he was still taller than Sanchia. "Yes, I am."

She darted a quick look at Gemma. "Does that mean you're married?"

Gemma sniffed and swiped at her eyes. "Not yet, but soon. You can be a bridesmaid."

Sanchia resumed her fascinated focus on Gabriel's face. "Are you really going to be my dad?"

"I am, and when I promise something, I do it."

There was a considering silence. "Okay." Sanchia beamed and slipped her hand in Gemma's. "You have to come inside now. Aunty Lauren's got a cake and Benny and Owen are driving her crazy 'cos they can't have any till you come."

Sanchia bounced as they walked. Now that the introductions were over, all her solemnity was gone. "It's chocolate. My fav'rit."

"Mine, too." Gabriel's eyes met Gemma's, his expression unreadable, and in that moment it clicked that Gabriel was at his most expressionless when he felt the most.

It wasn't much to go on, it didn't change the limbo they seemed to be caught in, but finally she had a kernel of hope to cling to. She didn't know if Gabriel could love her back the way she needed him to—she knew she couldn't make him love her—but for Sanchia's sake she had to try.

Just before they reached the steps, Gemma saw the moment Sanchia slipped her hand into Gabriel's and closed the small distance between them.

Her heart squeezed almost painfully tight as she saw Gabriel's fingers gently tighten around his daughter's, saw the expression on his face.

He loved her already.

At least that part was right.

After a walk on the beach, during which Gabriel got to spend some one-on-one time with Sanchia, who insisted on wearing the pink tutu over her orange bike shorts, they collected their daughter's things. Lauren and Sanchia's cousins waved them off, and ten minutes later they drove between the gates of the Messena estate.

Gabriel's gaze touched on hers as he braked on the gravel outside the front entrance. "Mom's still on Medinos, so we'll have the house to ourselves for a day or two at least."

Relief eased some of Gemma's tension. It was an odd enough feeling to be staying at the Messena's palatial family home, but she definitely wasn't looking forward to facing Gabriel's mother. As well as she knew Luisa Messena, she couldn't forget that she was not the bride Luisa had been certain Gabriel was waiting for.

Gabriel showed her and Sanchia to their rooms, which had been made up for them by the housekeeper, a Mrs. Sargent. Sanchia's room contained a collection of soft toys and a large wicker basket of toys that looked like it had seen hard service over the years. Gemma left Sanchia happily sorting through the toys while Gabriel showed her to her room, which was next door.

Pushing open the door, he stepped back so she could enter first. Gemma's heart pounded just a little faster as she walked into the room. Instead of the masculine setting she had expected, the room was pretty in white with touches of pink and green that created a fresh springlike effect. Clearly a room designed for feminine occupancy.

Gabriel carried her case over to an elegant freestanding wardrobe. "My room is at the end of the hall."

Gemma dragged her gaze from the way the white T-shirt clung across Gabriel's shoulders, revealing tanned biceps, the faint mark of Sanchia's sticky fingers on the pristine white interlock. Despite the hot afternoon at the beach, sand and ice cream and kids running in every direction, Gabriel's gaze was just as remote as it had been that morning when he had found out about Sanchia.

She set her handbag down on a pretty padded blanket box at the foot of the bed and watched while Gabriel unlatched the French doors that led out onto a terrace that ran along this side of the house.

Instantly, a warm breeze wafted inside, bringing with it the rich scents of the wisteria and the climbing rose that clambered up over the wrought-iron balustrade.

After hooking the door back, Gabriel stepped back inside the room, long lean fingers raking windblown hair out of his face. "Sanchia's door is locked, so she can't access the terrace, but even if she does, the balustrading is childproofed and the climbing rose has serious thorns. Most kids won't go near it."

"Thank you for being so good with Sanchia."

"It wasn't hard." He leaned one broad shoulder against the frame of the French doors, looking broodingly introspective and ultrasexy as he turned his head and stared out at the hot blue sky and the cool green of the trees in the distance. "Thank you for showing me those photographs of Sanchia this morning."

She shrugged and ran her hand over the pure white waffle duvet cover and a gorgeous quilted throw patterned with cabbage roses. "I have a lot more, and all the negatives if you want copies—"

"Since we'll be living together, I won't need copies."

The quiet timbre of his voice shivered through her, and in that moment it hit her forcibly that she was in a situation she thought she would never be in. She was engaged to Gabriel and staying in his mother's beautiful house. When they went back to Auckland after the wedding, she and Sanchia would be moving into Gabriel's apartment. Although he had made it clear enough that, for now, at least, they wouldn't be sharing a bed.

A wedding.

Disorientation mixed with a potent shot of misery made her mood drop like a stone. She had gotten through the day, smiled for Lauren and the kids and gotten over the hump of explaining that she and Gabriel not only had a future, they had a past. But the happiness she had tried to project over her engagement had been an empty thing.

The engagement was now real, but that special something, the possibility of a once-in-a-lifetime passionate love that had made her heart pound and her mood spiral crazily, as if she was a dizzy teenager, had gone.

They were together, but the relationship felt stiff and forced. She was miserably uncertain if Gabriel even wanted her anymore, and she guessed that was the essence of the problem. She needed to be loved and nurtured, to be the center of Gabriel's life. Most of all, she needed *him* to fall head over heels in love with her, but that was hardly possible if Gabriel felt forced to love her.

Gabriel straightened away from the doorjamb. "Hey. Don't look so depressed."

She drew a quick breath as he strolled toward her. "It's hard not to."

"I've made some preliminary arrangements for the wedding. Money's no object. Anything you want, we can do. The only constriction is time. For the dress, we can fly you anywhere you need to go, or have the dress, and the designer, flown to you."

The thought that Gabriel had the power to bring not only a dress, but the designer, to her briefly diverted her. She had been brought up to sew her own clothes, and that had always been a passion, but with the wedding so close she would have to buy dresses for both her and Sanchia.

Gabriel pulled out his wallet and extracted a platinum card. "You should take this. Order in what you want, and if you have any trouble let either me or Maris know."

The card, access to Gabriel's personal bank account, brought home both the reality and the underlying wrongness of their wedding.

She had agreed to marry Gabriel, but she was still shaky about the whole idea of marrying without the in-love factor. Using his credit card somehow seemed another big step into the relationship that she wasn't prepared for, another cold layer of necessity. "How do I use this?"

"Since you're not a signatory on the account yet, I'll have to give you my PIN."

He checked out a small writing bureau in one corner of the room, found a pen and a piece of paper and wrote a series of numbers in strong, slanting strokes.

"What if I lose the PIN? Or the card?"

He went curiously still. "I guess I'll try and weather the loss."

She suddenly felt a little ridiculous. Of course, he was a banker. He owned a bank. He could lose a thousand platinum cards and not notice it.

He handed her the slip of paper. "If you don't want to keep a written record, you'll have to memorize it."

She studied the four digits. Gabriel may be a banker,

but she had been a PA. "I have a good memory. I can still remember Zane's PIN, although he's probably changed it by now."

Gabriel's gaze narrowed. "Do we have to talk about Zane?"

A sharp little tingle ran through her at the irritable note in his voice.

Was that a hint of jealousy?

She took a deep breath and let it out slowly. "Zane who?"

He grinned quick and hard and caught her hand, drawing her close, and suddenly the terrible cold distance was gone. "Zane's a relative. When we're married, we'll bump into him from time to time."

Her palms flattened against his chest, and she found herself staring into the dark, chocolate-brown depths of his eyes, happily mesmerized by the gold striations that gave them an amber gleam, the long silky curl of his lashes. "You don't have to worry about Zane. He was my boss, and a friend, that's all."

"Good. Because I don't share."

The possessive note in his voice sparked even more hope. That morning she had thought Gabriel would end up hating her for keeping Sanchia from him, that with their engagement charade morphing into a marriage of convenience he would have a difficult time even wanting her. But for the first time since she had walked into Gabriel's sitting room and realized that he knew Sanchia was his, she thought they really did have a chance.

He brushed the delicate skin beneath one eye with a fingertip. "You look tired. You should get some rest."

Cupping her face, he dipped his head and touched his mouth to hers, but to Gemma the kiss felt perfunctory and forced, as if his mind was on other things. Despite the positivity of a few seconds ago, her doubts came crashing back.

If Gabriel had found her so easy to resist six years ago, what were the chances that he would really, honestly fall for her now?

The reality was that the only solid link between them was Sanchia.

On cue, Sanchia skipped into the room. Instantly, Gabriel let her go. All shyness gone now, Sanchia produced her phone from a small zip pocket in her jacket and requested Gabriel's number.

Sending Gemma a bemused look, Gabriel extracted his phone and sat down on the blanket box. Automatically, Sanchia clambered up beside him, her legs dangling, inches short of the floor.

Sitting together, Gemma couldn't help noticing that they looked heartbreakingly alike. Once again feeling ridiculously vulnerable and isolated, Gemma busied herself unpacking while Gabriel and Sanchia swapped numbers. As she hung a dress in the wardrobe, she was aware of Gabriel leaving then Sanchia's stifled giggle.

Out in the hall a cell phone buzzed, and Gabriel's footsteps stopped dead. Gemma heard the low timbre of his voice as he answered the call, followed by Sanchia's delighted answer.

Gemma kept hanging clothes then walked through to Sanchia's room to help settle her in.

Gabriel had bonded with Sanchia in the space of a few hours. And he had kissed Gemma. There was hope.

More than hope. Last night with Gabriel had been beyond sublime; it had been heartbreakingly special. There was no reason it couldn't happen again, and the way things had gone today, it needed to.

She pulled out a silky peach chemise pooled in the bottom of her case. Unzipping a side pocket, she removed the magazine with the article on seduction that she'd kept.

If she could talk herself into seducing Zane, a man she had only ever liked, not loved, she could seduce her husband-to-be.

Tonight.

Moonlight gently illumined the night sky as Gabriel strolled out onto the balcony, the soft black cotton pants he'd pulled on after his shower clinging low on his hips, a towel draped over one shoulder.

Without the benefit of the slowly swishing ceiling fan in his room, it was hotter outside than in, the scents of wisteria and roses and night jessamine infusing the air with a cloying richness. A far cry from the stormy night on Medinos he was having trouble forgetting and the passionate hours from last night that were still etched on his brain.

He paced restlessly along his end of the deck, taking care to avoid Gemma's room.

He wasn't desperate—yet.

Although that was a mantra that was rapidly losing its power.

Soft music drifted on the night air, the low throaty sound of a blues singer. Frowning, he glanced in the direction of Gemma's room and noticed that both of her French doors were open.

Jaw tight, he strolled toward his room, which just happened to take him closer to Gemma's.

A rich, musky scent that reminded him of a dark, expensive little souk he'd once walked through in Morroco—and which had been filled with filmy lace garments, interesting bits of leather and shelves of aphrodisiacs—caught at his nostrils, drawing him past his door.

Gemma stepped out onto the balcony, almost stopping

his heart. Dressed in a sexy little chemise that revealed an enticing swell of cleavage and left her long legs mostly bare, she took his breath. "I thought you were tired."

She shrugged. "I had a nap earlier—" She frowned. "Darn, that didn't sound good."

Another step and he could see that the scent came from flickering candles set on almost every available surface of Gemma's room. "What's wrong with taking a nap if you're tired?"

Although he could barely concentrate on the conversation. The musky scent from the candles and the seductive setting they created were distracting him, but not as much as the fierce response of his body.

"Because it sounds like something a tired mother might do."

"And you're not that?"

"Not tonight." Stepping close, she grasped both ends of the towel draped around his neck and pulled him into her room, step by slow step. Every muscle in his body tightened at the slumberous seduction in her gaze, and then he saw the magazine.

It wasn't folded open, but he recognized that it was unmistakeably the same one that contained the article "How To Seduce Your Man in Ten Easy Moves."

Relief that they had finally moved past the awkward silences of the day eased some of his tension.

From memory, Gemma had settled on the section headed Slow, Heated Enticements.

If he wasn't mistaken, he was about to be embroiled in technique number six: setting the scene for seduction with erotic scented candles.

Despite his arousal, the fact that Gemma thought she needed to seduce him didn't please Gabriel. It reminded him of her seduction attempt with Zane, that when she had needed a husband, and a father for Sanchia, Gemma hadn't approached him.

He was fighting jealousy, pure and simple. He wanted Gemma to be upfront with him and spontaneous. He wanted the same heart-pounding passion he had gotten just days ago on Medinos, and last night in Gemma's apartment.

His stomach tightened on the thought that maybe this seduction wasn't for his benefit so much as Gemma's. She had agreed to marriage but, despite admitting that she had loved him in the past, he didn't know how she really felt now.

Gemma let go of the towel. "What's wrong?"

He picked up the magazine. "This." Stepping out on the balcony, he tossed it over the side. "We didn't need that six years ago. We don't need it now."

Gemma, who had followed him out onto the balcony, stared over the side as the fluttering magazine hit the pavers around the pool. "You went through my bag on Medinos."

"While you were asleep. And before you ask why, it was because I was jealous." He caught her around the waist and drew her close. "If I'd found condoms I would have punched Zane out."

He saw the instant glimmer of relief in her eyes and his mood lightened. That was spontaneous and her relief that he was jealous was definitely real.

Her palms, which were spread on his chest, slipped up as she coiled her arms around his neck. "I'm sorry about the magazine. It was a dumb idea all around. I should have tossed it on Medinos."

Her body slid against his, and his hands closed on her hips. News flash, he thought grimly, she did not need the magazine.

She frowned, her gaze startlingly direct. "Do you still want to make love?"

"Just as long as you don't think you're giving me some kind of consolation prize," he growled.

She smiled, the kind of wide smile that stopped his heart.

He pulled her close enough that she could feel just exactly how much he did want to make love to her. "Just promise me one thing." He picked up a handful of silky hair, threading his fingers through it. "Do whatever it is you do and make this red again."

"You don't like brunettes?"

Swinging her up in his arms he carried her to the bed, set her down and joined her. "Not for six years."

"Then I might consider it."

He watched as she slipped out of the chemise, restraining himself from simply grabbing her and taking control. His patience was rewarded as she slowly peeled his soft cotton pants over his hips and down his legs.

When he was finally naked she straddled him and produced a foil packet and ripped it open. He almost grinned when he saw the condom, which was color coordinated with the candles, although the desire to smile disappeared as she ripped open the foil package and began to fit the condom. The feel of her hands on him and the small fumbling movements she made almost drove him insane.

When he was completely sheathed, she gently lowered herself onto him. Taking a deep breath, he fought for control as she accustomed herself to having him inside her then began to move, slowly and smoothly, closing her eyes as she did so.

Exquisite pleasure rolled through Gabriel. He framed Gemma's hips, steadying her as the tension coiled and built on endless waves of heat until, with a muttered expletive,

Gabriel moved, rolling her beneath him as the shimmering heat and intensity coiled tight and the scented, candlelit night dissolved in a blaze of light.

Fifteen

The wedding was set for the following weekend, the reception booked at the Dolphin Bay Resort, which was adjacent to the Messena estate.

Luisa arrived home after two days, but happily Gabriel had already explained the whole situation to his mother over the phone. Sanchia took care of any other awkwardness. As the long-awaited first Messena grandchild, she was always guaranteed center stage for Luisa. Gemma was more than happy to take a quiet step back and let Luisa come to terms with the impending marriage.

The following day, after another night of lovemaking and physical closeness, during which the distance she couldn't seem to close was just as present, just as frustrating, Gabriel had to go back to town for an appointment he couldn't cancel.

Already dressed for work in a dark suit with a blue tie

that made him look formal and distant, Gabriel pulled her close for a kiss, then picked Sanchia up and hugged her.

Standing on the forecourt, waving goodbye as he drove away, Gemma couldn't help comparing his response to Sanchia with his response to her.

With Sanchia there was no ambivalence. Gabriel loved her unconditionally; it was there in the teasing exchanges, the way he relaxed with his daughter. His response to her was guarded; there was no other word for it. No matter how hard she tried, the tension hadn't entirely dissolved.

While Gabriel was away, Gemma threw herself into ordering the dresses for the wedding. Luisa, who was expert at all forms of entertaining, took over the organizing for the pre-wedding dinner and the ceremony and reception the next day.

Expecting the wedding to be very small because of the short notice, Gemma was a little dismayed to see the Messena social network come to immediate vibrant life. Family and friends were not only coming from distant places in New Zealand, Gabriel had organized charter flights to bring cousins and relatives from overseas.

As she spent time with Gabriel's mother, Gemma came to the conclusion that, in her own way, Luisa was trying to make her feel at home and accepted as Gabriel's bride.

Warmed, when the dresses were delivered by helicopter on the front lawn, she unwrapped the parcels and showed Luisa the wedding and flower girl dresses she had selected.

Luisa touched the silk and exclaimed over the workmanship. "I trained as a seamstress before I got married, so I know how much work has gone into these. They're beautiful. If you need any help with the fitting, I can do the alterations."

Touched by Luisa's kindness, the days passed almost too quickly.

* * *

Gabriel returned from Auckland the day before the wedding and an hour before the pre-wedding function Luisa had planned at the Dolphin Bay Resort was due to start.

His cell rang as he walked into the front hall. Setting down Sanchia, who had rushed out to chatter excitedly at him, he fielded the call, his expression grim.

By the time he got off the phone, Gemma was on the phone talking to her best friend, Elena, Zane's current PA, who had just arrived in Dolphin Bay.

The private moment she had been hoping to share with Gabriel slipped away. Instead, Gabriel sent her another one of the neutral glances that frightened her to death because they made her feel that, emotionally, he was growing even more distant, and strode up the stairs to his room.

Ten minutes later, he appeared, showered and dressed in a pair of dark trousers and a gauzy dark shirt worn loose, the two top buttons undone. The effect was casual, devastating. Hot.

When he got close to her, instead of kissing her, he reached into his pocket and brought out a pair of diamond earrings. "You should wear these tonight."

The earrings were beautiful, part of the Fabergé set that matched her engagement ring and necklace.

He cupped her bare shoulders, the warmth of his palms sending a hot tingle through her as he turned her so she could see herself in the large oval mirror that was hung just inside the door.

Lifting her hair away from one ear, sending more shivering-hot whispers of sensation through her, he dangled an earring so she could see the effect. "Perfect."

Although, Gemma wasn't looking at the earring. It was Gabriel's gaze she was most interested in, but the emotion, the warmth she longed to see, wasn't there.

Misery twisted in her as she took the earrings and began very carefully putting them on. Originally they would have been clip-ons, but someone had thoughtfully had them converted for pierced ears.

They dangled, scintillating with the same pure fire as her ring, perfectly matching her pink dress and making her look like a million dollars. "They're beautiful, but you don't have to give me gifts. The ring is more than enough."

He turned her around, and this time he did kiss her. "You're going to be my wife. You'll have to get used to wearing expensive jewelry." His mouth quirked at one corner, the first hint of humor she'd seen from him since he'd arrived and in that moment she realized how grim he'd been. "Unfortunately, as a banker's wife, it's part of the job."

The party was elegant but casual, held mostly outside under an enormous white tent that would also be used for the wedding reception the following day.

Gabriel circulated with Gemma, introducing her to the family and friends she didn't know and keeping a wary eye on Sanchia, who was running wild with a couple of her cousins. As night fell, the music got a little louder and the resort lights glowed to life, shimmering off a huge curvaceous swimming pool and spotlighting clumps of graceful palms.

As they walked together, Gemma seemed more than ordinarily quiet, but he put that down to tiredness. According to Luisa, Sanchia had been fretful at night, so Gemma had missed sleep. Add to that the workload of organizing the wedding and he would be surprised if she was in sparkling form. Still...

Movement registered in the parking lot. He frowned as he noticed the dark head of a new arrival.

Zane Atraeus. Fury gripped Gabriel. He could hardly believe it. Moments later, Zane disappeared, swallowed up by the crowd spilling out of the marquee.

Excusing himself, he left Gemma chatting with her friend Elena as they watched the kids playing and strode toward the last place he had seen Zane.

He found him standing at the bar with Nick. Suppressing the primitive urge to grip Zane's shoulder and spin him around, Gabriel contented himself with asking Zane if they could have a word in private.

Zane lifted a brow, but didn't argue. "If you're worried about Gemma, I never touched her."

"I know that." Gabriel clamped down on his impatience. "What I wanted to know is what you plan on doing next."

Zane's gaze narrowed. "That would be marrying the woman I love, in about two months time."

Gabriel let out a breath. He knew Zane; he was a straight shooter and not given to displays of emotions. If he said he was in love, he was in love, period. "Did Gemma ever date anyone other than you?"

"Not that I know of."

A stunning brunette Gabriel recognized as Lilah Cole strolled toward them and slid her arm around Zane's waist. He pulled her in close.

Zane made introductions.

Gabriel noticed the engagement ring on Lilah's finger. "Congratulations."

Lilah smiled. "Likewise. Looks like weddings are in the air."

Zane tucked Lilah in more snugly against his side. "I do know one thing about Gemma. She had plenty of opportunities to date. Guys hit on her all the time, and I mean all the time. Usually, she didn't want to know. If you ask me, she's waiting for that once-in-a-lifetime special love."

Gabriel didn't miss the challenge in Zane's words, or the steely glance that went with them. Not quite a warning, but close.

In that moment, he warmed to his cousin more than he ever had. Zane had genuinely cared about Gemma, and he was sending Gabriel a curt message that he would hear about it if she got hurt.

Zane's opinion that Gemma was looking for true love reverberated through Gabriel as he watched his cousin and Lilah stroll over to the buffet, and suddenly he got her.

Gemma was an idealist and a romantic. Nothing else explained the extremity of her actions. She was looking for true love, but she was also wary of being hurt.

For years he had tried to keep tabs on her. He had been constantly frustrated, because she would disappear overseas with Zane, or she wouldn't be at the social event he had decided to attend because she was there.

It hadn't been pure coincidence that he had never managed to connect with her. She had been actively avoiding him.

He hadn't understood why. Now that he knew about Sanchia, he did. Gemma hadn't wanted to be forced into a compromised relationship. She had been protecting herself, her daughter *and him*.

Not because she didn't love him, but because she did.

"Gabriel."

A familiar feminine voice that lately had started to intrude just a little too often into his life jerked his head around. "Simone." His stomach sank. "You weren't supposed to come here."

A movement at the periphery of his vision distracted him. He frowned, for a moment certain he had seen a flash of the ivory-toned dress Gemma had been wearing. Although he had probably been mistaken. With the number of women and men wearing light, cool colors, it could have been anyone.

Simone placed a hand on his arm. "I couldn't stay away. I had to see you."

His jaw tightened at her sudden intensity. An intensity he had been avoiding at work for weeks now. He removed her fingers. "You were supposed to be on holiday this week."

"I am." She smiled with the same kind of steely determination he had seen on her very wealthy father's face when he closed a deal that he wanted. "I'm here, in Dolphin Bay. I just checked into the resort."

Gemma froze in place behind the tree she had ducked behind when she had seen Simone. Her cool, light voice, and the words, "I couldn't stay away, I had to see you," kept reverberating through her mind.

And it wasn't just the words, but the way they were spoken, with an edge of desperation.

She shifted back into the shadows at the side of the tent as Gabriel walked with Simone into the resort.

Simone looked as cool and perfect as she had at the bank, although distinctly bridal with the white shell dress and discreet pearls. Gabriel was being careful not to touch her, but his distance and stiffness was revealing.

"You weren't supposed to come here."

The words indicated that there had been a conversation, probably during the important appointment Gabriel hadn't been able to miss in Auckland that week. He would have had to tell Simone that they could no longer be together because he was marrying the mother of his child.

Feeling numb, she went into the hotel lounge that was open to the party, turned down a corridor that led to the ladies' room, which also contained a business center.

Pushing the door of the business center open, she stepped inside and walked to one of the desks. Extracting her phone from her bag, which had a sizable screen and an internet connection, she went online and did a search using Simone's name.

The second hit was all she needed. It was a gossip columnist's piece about a charity event Simone had attended with Gabriel, ending with speculation about an expected engagement before the end of the month.

Gemma stared at the photo of Gabriel and Simone together and the caption beneath—The Perfect Couple.

The article explained the conversation she had overheard on Medinos, when Luisa Messena had talked about an engagement by the end of the month. The date of the charity event was less than three weeks ago.

She did a further search and found more information. Simone's family was rich and connected, which made sense of why Gabriel hadn't asked Simone to pose as his fake fiancée. He probably hadn't gotten to the stage of proposing, so to ask that of Simone would have been totally wrong.

Gemma didn't think Gabriel was in love with Simone, otherwise he wouldn't have made love with her. But neither had he ever said he was in love with Gemma.

What really mattered was that the very thing Gabriel hadn't wanted to happen, had. Six years ago he'd had to put aside any plans and dreams he might have had to take over the business and responsibility for his family. Now she had taken away the one free choice he had left.

She'd dreamed of marrying him six years ago, but because he loved her, not because he was fulfilling yet another duty, another obligation.

And if she didn't do something, they would get married tomorrow and head for an even bigger disaster.

Closing down the page and her internet connection, she tucked the phone back in her bag and walked slowly back through the lounge and out onto the hotel terrace.

The sound of the music, which before had seemed just right, now seemed overloud, sparking a sharp ache at her temples, and the number of people at the party seemed to have swelled.

Fingers tightening on her clutch, Gemma searched the laughing, chatting groups of guests and tried to think. Gabriel was nowhere in sight; neither was Simone.

The thought that they could be in Simone's room, since she had checked into the resort, sent a sharp pain straight to her heart, although she quickly vetoed the idea. She knew Gabriel, and he was honorable. She wouldn't love him if he were a low-down sneaky womanizer.

He would be talking to Simone and trying to get her to leave without making a scene. Maybe he would even be helping her check out, then he would make sure she left.

She knew from the things that Luisa had said that Gabriel was meticulous about detail. When he took care of a situation he left no stone unturned. That was why he had made such a success of the bank, despite being thrown in the deep end when his father had died.

He would be finishing things with Simone so that there would be no repercussions within their marriage. But it was too late, because the one flaw in her thinking had been exposed. Her own emotions were the problem. The second Gabriel had suggested they get married, she should have vetoed the idea and suggested they just share custody of Sanchia.

But no. She'd seen Gabriel fall in love with Sanchia and crumbled and selfishly grabbed at what she had wanted.

Walking quickly, she made her way back to the last place she had seen her sister Lauren and asked her if she could have Sanchia for the night.

Lauren frowned. "What's wrong? You're white as a sheet."

Gemma made an effort to smile. "I'm okay, just a little tired."

Lauren shook her head. "What am I saying? Of course you're tired. You helped organize this lovely party, and you're getting married tomorrow. Of course we'll have Sanchia."

Finding Elena was a little more difficult; she seemed to have melted away. Gemma checked her wristwatch. It had been a good fifteen minutes since she had seen Gabriel and Simone disappear into the resort lobby. By the time she had searched the marquee another good ten minutes had passed. She didn't know how long Gabriel would spend with Simone, but if he was trying to check her out of the resort it wouldn't take too long.

Eventually, she saw Elena, distinctive in her red dress, her hair a dark swath down her back, in conversation with a shadowy masculine figure at the deserted end of the pool nearest the resort parking lot. For a moment, she thought it was Gabriel, and her stomach tightened until she recognized one of Gabriel's brothers.

As she approached, he dragged long fingers through his hair, as if frustrated, then turned, letting her know that he was aware his conversation with Elena was no longer private.

Light glanced off one taut cheekbone and a stubbled, obdurate jaw, and highlighted caramel streaks in his tousled dark hair. Super-sexy and hot, but not Gabriel. It was his younger brother, Nick.

Taking a deep breath, Gemma broke into a conversation that looked unusually fraught.

Elena shot her a turbulent look, her dark eyes still lit with the remnants of some fiery emotion. The display of temper was distinctly out of character, because normally Elena was ultracalm and controlled. She was the kind of woman who had a walk-in closet for shoes and bespoke designed hangers for scarves and belts. When put against the cheerful chaos of Gemma's wardrobe, that kind of control spoke volumes.

Gemma glanced at Nick and wondered what she had walked into. "Hello, Nick, sorry to butt in, but I need Elena."

His normally warm green eyes were glacial. "Join the queue."

Elena shot Nick an irritated look. "Last time I looked there wasn't a queue." Pointedly, she turned to Gemma. "It's okay, I can come now. I'm all finished here."

Nick frowned. "We need to talk."

Elena gave him a bland smile Gemma recognized only too well—the pacifying smile of a PA for a difficult client. "It's too late for another discussion tonight."

Nick sent her a cool, measuring look. "Then save me a dance at the wedding."

Gemma led the way into the parking lot and found a quiet spot under the deep shadow of a pohutukawa tree.

Elena made a seat for herself on the low plastered wall that separated the parking lot from the sweeping lawns. "One night and he thinks I'm a doormat."

Gemma almost dropped the diamond earrings she had just carefully extracted from her lobes. "You slept with Nick Messena?"

"It was a long time ago. A youthful mistake. Everyone's entitled to one."

Her thinking exactly. One mistake was allowable, not two.

She took a deep breath. "I need your help."

Sixteen

Gabriel checked his watch as he saw Simone into her car and waited until her taillights disappeared down the drive. Feeling grimly annoyed at the pressure both Simone and her socialite mother had brought to bear, both personally and through the press, he headed back to the party.

After several minutes of walking through the crowded marquee and pool area, he stepped into the lobby of the resort and saw Elena.

The minute he started to ask her if she knew where Gemma was, he knew something was wrong.

Gemma had seen him with Simone and totally misread the situation. "Where is she?"

Elena reached into her evening bag and took out a folded envelope. "I don't know. I'm sorry I can't be more helpful. I tried to stop her, but she said she needed some time. She gave me this to hand to you."

Gabriel opened the envelope. His stomach dropped

when he saw the engagement ring and the earrings. "How long ago did she leave?"

"A few minutes."

Gabriel headed straight for the parking lot. Gemma wouldn't leave without Sanchia, which meant that they could have gone to the house to get some things before they left Dolphin Bay.

He climbed into his car, thumbing a number on his phone as he slammed the door. A quick conversation later and he knew that neither Gemma nor Sanchia had gone to the house.

As he accelerated down the drive, he tried Gemma's phone, without much hope. Even if her phone was turned on, when she saw his number she probably wouldn't answer it. When the call went through to voice mail, he tossed the phone on the passenger seat and continued driving.

He turned into Lauren's drive on the off chance that Gemma's sister would know something. When Lauren answered the door and told him that she had Sanchia tucked up in bed, all the breath left his lungs.

"Are you all right?"

He met Lauren's concerned gaze. "She's left."

"Left?" Lauren frowned. "She wouldn't. She loves you. She always has."

Gabriel's fingers curled into fists. "What makes you say that?"

As far as he was concerned, apart from the one mistake he had made years ago in leaving Gemma, she had been the one walking away.

"You do know she's only ever slept with you, right?"

Gabriel's jaw clamped. "Yes."

"Do you know why a girl as gorgeous as Gemma has only ever slept with you? It's because she fell in love with you when she was about sixteen and, somehow, being Gemma, she just never fell out of love."

There it was again, the extremity. He knew about it, had tried to reason it out, but in a blinding moment he realized there was nothing to reason.

She loved him. It was black and white, an absolute truth.

He stared out into the moonlit night, edgy frustration eating at him because he needed to find her now. "Have you got any idea where she would have gone?"

Lauren frowned. "If she's running out on the wedding, I'd say back to Auckland."

Not with Sanchia still here.

And suddenly he knew. Gemma was a romantic and an idealist. *She loved him.* There was only one place she would be.

He drew a deep breath. "I think I know where she is."

Gemma carried her shoes as she waded the last few yards to the island that sat just south of the resort.

The tide was on its way in. As she'd walked, waves had kept splashing against the narrow causeway, gradually soaking her. To make matters worse, a thick bank of cloud had moved in, obscuring the moonlight so that she'd had to pick her way carefully, in case she missed the causeway and fell into the deeper water on either side.

The water now almost entirely covered the causeway. A few more minutes and it would disappear under the waves and the island would be cut off from the mainland.

Stepping onto the pretty, hard-packed shell beach, she set down her evening bag and the bottle of water she'd taken from the marquee drinks table, and used the resort towel she'd borrowed from the pool house to dry herself off.

As she straightened, her phone chimed. Taking the

phone out of her clutch, she checked the number, her heart thumping hard in her chest when she saw that Gabriel was trying to call her.

The call went through to voice mail.

Resolutely she turned the phone off. Slipping it back into her bag, she picked up her shoes, the bag and the water and kept walking, and wished she had thought to borrow a flashlight.

Ten minutes of careful negotiation of the rock-strewn beach later, she rounded a small headland and found the pretty resort beach house. Although in reality it was little more than a pavilion that was used for day-trippers and sometimes for evening events like champagne picnics.

She stepped into the trellised shelter with its graceful pergola-style roof and padded daybeds and sat down. Silence enclosed her, broken by the gentle rhythm of the sea as waves broke on the sand, and more distantly, the lonely cry of a pukeko, a native swamp bird that roamed the area around the resort.

Now that she was here, the idea of escaping to a place where Gabriel could choose to come and find her if he truly wanted to seemed desperate and hopelessly flawed.

For one thing, she hadn't thought about the tide. Walking here wouldn't be an option until the small hours of the morning. Even if he did remember the place where it had all begun for them, he wouldn't be able to get here unless he managed to borrow a boat.

She was going to have a long, lonely night, and then she would have to face the music tomorrow.

Sanchia was expecting to be a bridesmaid. There were people coming from Sydney, Florida, London and Medinos for the wedding. Luisa had insisted on ordering a hopelessly extravagant and utterly gorgeous six-tiered cake, with chocolate layers for the kids.

Gabriel would be... She drew a sudden breath. Gabriel would be hurt.

The lonely quiet seemed to seep into her skin. Maybe she wasn't Gabriel's dream come true as a wife, but he had been ready to commit, and he wanted to be a father to Sanchia.

Pushing to her feet she walked back down onto the beach and began to pace. No matter which way she looked at the situation and the decisions she'd made, first to agree to the marriage, then to get cold feet and run out on it, she had made a mess of things.

Half an hour later, beginning to feel desperate because now she wanted off the island and there was no way that was going to happen, she walked back to the pavilion and looked for her phone.

She thumbed through to contacts and pressed Gabriel's number. Holding her breath, she listened to the ring tone, her mood plummeting even further when the call wasn't picked up.

She gave it a couple of minutes while she walked down to the break line and tried again. The phone rang several times. Misery gripping her, she stared up at the dull, leaden sky. "Pick up, Gabriel. Where are you when I need you?"

"I'm here," a low rough voice said. "Talk to me, babe, before I go crazy."

Gemma spun. Gabriel was just meters away, hair slicked back, bronzed torso gleaming with moisture as if he'd not long ago walked out of the surf. His dark pants were just as wet, clinging to his narrow hips and sticking to his skin where they touched.

For a bleak moment she thought she was hallucinating. "You swam."

"It was farther than I thought." He pulled a dripping cell out of his pocket. "No point in ringing that number again. The phone's dead."

And suddenly she didn't care about Simone or any of the other beautiful, intelligent women in his life, and she didn't care about the old inferiority complex that had crippled her for so long. Gabriel was here, now, for her.

He was soaking wet and his phone was destroyed *because he'd had to swim to get to her.*

And suddenly she saw him, not the wealthy banker with platinum cards and gleaming Maseratis, but the gorgeous, beleaguered, beautiful man she loved.

He just had time to toss the phone in the sand before she caromed into his chest.

His arms closed around her, hauling her in tight. "I wasn't sure that you wanted me to follow."

"I did. I do. I'm sorry I ran out on you like that. I can't believe you came after me."

His gaze locked on hers, dark and emotion-filled. "Then you don't know me very well. I haven't seriously wanted anyone but you for years. Why do you think I'm still single?" He paused for breath. "Marry me."

"In a heartbeat."

He cupped her face. "Promise?"

"On my heart. I love you, no one else. I've loved you for years." And finally she blurted out the problem that had hampered her all those years ago. "I thought I wasn't good enough. I was an employee."

He gave her the kind of mystified look that told her that she had been completely wrong on that score. "I'll admit that the employee thing was a problem just after Dad died, because of the press. But the real reason I stayed away from you was because what I felt was so addictive, I was afraid I'd make the same mistake my father had. I knew I couldn't do the job that needed to be done and have a relationship with you at the same time."

Compulsively, she ran her hands over his shoulders, curled her fingers into the damp hair at his nape. Despite the fact that he was wet and should be cold, his skin was warm, the life in him burning bright and indomitable.

She cupped his jaw, loving the grim masculinity of his five o'clock shadow, needing the reassurance of touch. She was hardly able to believe that he was here, when she had done her level best to mess everything up.

He held one hand captive and turned his mouth against it in a gentle caress. "I know you saw me with Simone. She was trying to maneuver me into a relationship. I wasn't interested, but she couldn't take no for an answer."

"I thought you wanted her. I felt like I'd trapped you into marriage. I wanted to give you the choice."

"Where you're concerned, there's only been one choice for a long time. I'm sorry I let you go all those years ago. I won't let you go again." He paused, his voice husky with emotion. "I love you."

And in that moment the moon came out, spreading a molten silvery glow over sea and wet sand, glimmering on the damp, muscular curve of his shoulders and allowing her to see the softness in his gaze. Closing her eyes, Gemma lifted up on her toes and kissed him.

When she opened her eyes, Gabriel smiled, picked her up with the easy strength she loved and carried her into the pavilion.

When he set her down on one of the daybeds and joined her, she saw the time glowing on his watch. It was after midnight.

Their wedding day.

* * *

Hours later, Gemma woke to find the first gray light of dawn illuminating the pavilion. Shivering slightly, she cuddled in closer to Gabriel.

They'd made love, slept and made love again, then finally dragged two daybeds together for comfort, found a store of towels and beach blankets in a locker, and made a bed of sorts.

Gabriel caught a strand of her hair and tugged it lightly. "About Simone. I didn't have an appointment with her. We did have a discussion, but it was about the loan structure for a major development she was working on. She offered to bring it down personally for my signature. I told her not to bother. The reason I had to go back to Auckland was to sort out the legal paperwork dissolving Mario's trusteeship."

Gemma turned on her side and propped her chin on the heel of her hand. "I forgot completely about that."

Gabriel pulled her close and kissed her softly. "Forget the bank. I have. It's our wedding day."

Giddy delight shimmered through her. She could still scarcely believe that she and Gabriel were getting married after all, that she would wear her lovely wedding dress and walk down the aisle toward him. That Gabriel loved her with passion, and had for years.

The wedding was held in a pretty church on top of a hill, with a breathtaking view of Dolphin Bay.

Gemma was ready early. Her mother, Lauren and the kids and Elena had arrived just minutes before the influx of hairdressers and beauticians. She'd deliberately hurried each stage because the last thing she wanted to do was to make Gabriel wait.

After everything that had happened, all she wanted to do was get to the church early and get married to her man.

Her gown was gorgeous, dove-soft ivory silk that made her skin glow like honey and made her hair look even richer. The Fabergé diamonds went perfectly with the dress.

While she had dressed, Luisa had filled her in on the history of the jewels. Apparently, Gabriel's grandfather, Guido, had fallen in love with a Russian girl during the war. Separated by the conflict, he had continued to woo her with letters. When the replies had stopped, worried, he had gone to Russia and found her.

Destitute after the losses of the war, Eugenie had decided he wouldn't want her anymore. Guido Messena had proven otherwise. The jewels had been his wedding gift to her.

Luisa had given her a smiling glance at the end of the small story and Gemma had picked up on the subtext. Gabriel had known the romantic history of the jewels. He had chosen them for that reason.

When the bridal limousine arrived at the church, it was so early guests had to be hurried inside. Gabriel, who was outside the church talking with Nick and one of his other brothers, Kyle, glanced across at her and met her gaze for a heart-stopping moment.

Mesmerizingly handsome in a gray morning suit, instead of going inside the church with his brothers, Gabriel helped her out of the limousine, smiled into her eyes then took her arm.

When they reached the nave and the music began, Gemma stopped and waited for Elena to organize Sanchia, who was the flower girl.

When Gabriel didn't walk on and join Nick and Kyle at the altar, but stayed with them, waiting for the wedding march to begin, she sent him an anxious look. "They're waiting for you at the altar."

In response he took her arm, drawing her close to his side as Sanchia began her careful trek to the altar, tossing rose petals. "They can wait. Right now I'm going to walk up the aisle with my two girls."

* * * * *

A sneaky peek at next month...

Desire™

PASSIONATE AND DRAMATIC LOVE STORIES

My wish list for next month's titles...

In stores from 21st June 2013:

☐ Rumour Has It – Maureen Child

& A Very Exclusive Engagement
  – Andrea Laurence

2 stories in each book - only £5.49!

☐ The Texan's Contract Marriage – Sara Orwig

& A Baby Between Friends – Kathie DeNosky

☐ Temptation on His Terms – Robyn Grady

& Taming the Lone Wolff – Janice Maynard

Available at WHSmith, Tesco, Asda, Eason, Amazon and Apple

Just can't wait?

Visit us Online

You can buy our books online a month before they hit the shops! **www.millsandboon.co.uk**

0613/51

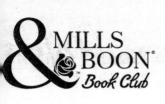

Join the Mills & Boon Book Club

Want to read more **Desire**™ books?
We're offering you **2 more** absolutely **FREE!**

We'll also treat you to these fabulous extras:

- 🌹 Exclusive offers and much more!

- 🌹 FREE home delivery

- 🌹 FREE books and gifts with our special rewards scheme

Get your free books now!

visit www.millsandboon.co.uk/bookclub
or call Customer Relations on 020 8288 2888